FIGHTING THE ODDS

KRISTEN GRANATA

MORE FROM KRISTEN

The Collision Series Box Set with Bonus Epilogue
Collision: Book 1
Avoidance: Book 2, Sequel
The Other Brother: Book 3, Standalone
Fighting the Odds: Book 4, Standalone
Hating the Boss: Book 1, Standalone
Inevitable: Contemporary standalone
What's Left of Me: Contemporary standalone
Dear Santa: Holiday novella
Someone You Love: Contemporary standalone

Want to gain access to exclusive news & giveaways?
Sign up for my monthly newsletter!

Visit my website: https://kristengranata.com/
Instagram: https://www.instagram.com/kristen_granata/
Facebook: https://www.facebook.com/kristen.granata.16
Twitter: https://twitter.com/kristen_granata

Want to be part of my KREW?

Join Kristen's Reading Emotional Warriors
A Facebook group where we can discuss my books, books you're
reading, and where friends will remind you what a badass warrior
you are.

Love bookish shirts, mugs, & accessories?
Shop my book merch shop!

This one's for you...
I know you're tired.
I know you're scared.
I know you want to give up.
Don't.
You are not alone.
Fight for happiness.
Fight for love.
Fight for the life you want.
Fight for yourself.
You can do this.
You deserve it.
You're a fucking warrior.

PLAYLIST

Carla's Playlist
Click here to listen to Carla's playlist on Spotify

TJ's Playlist
Click here to listen to TJ's playlist on Spotify

Chapter One

THE PRESENT

arla

WHAT DO YOU WANT?

To anyone else, it would've been an easy enough question to answer. People state what they want all the time. They voice it when ordering food; when buying a home; when choosing which college to attend. There are simple choices, like what to wear when getting dressed. There are more serious choices, like cremation versus casket. Telling people what we want is a necessary part of life. It's how we communicate.

I'd always considered myself someone who knows what she wants.

What do you want for dinner? Tacos.

Where do you want to go to college? Florida State.

How many kids do you want to have? Two.

Will you marry me? Yes.

I'd always communicated what I wanted and I'd always gotten it. Life was simple. Life was good. I was happy.

Two parallel lines on a pregnancy test changed everything.

Those lines shouldn't have changed a thing though. Did they throw me a curve ball? Of course. Did they make things a little more challenging? Absolutely. Should they have caused my fiancé to break up with me and throw away our future together? I didn't think so.

Joe and I were high school sweethearts. For four years, we planned what our lives would be like once we graduated. We'd move in together, attend the same college, and get engaged. Then we'd get married and have kids. I had it all written down on a list tacked to the corkboard in our bedroom. A list we'd made together.

After graduation, we moved into an off-campus apartment together and Joe asked me to marry him. Everything was going according to plan. Check, check, check. Our ducks waddled in a row. Getting pregnant mixed up the order of things, but it was still something we'd wanted.

Until we didn't want the same things anymore.

My nana always said, "You can never truly know someone." You think you do. You finish his sentences and anticipate his moves, like your favorite movie you've watched over and over. Until one day, you're standing in front of him, looking at him like he's a stranger. The words flowing from his mouth sound foreign to your ears, a language you can't seem to decipher no matter how hard you try. The warmth from his touch is no longer a comfort, but sends you crawling out of your skin.

"*I want you to get an abortion.*" He said it as easily as if he'd ordered a drink at the bar. *I'll have a rum and coke, and the lady will have an abortion.*

He told me to choose. It was him or the baby. Making that choice was the hardest decision I'd ever made, but it wasn't because I didn't know what I wanted. I knew, even then.

I chose to keep the baby.

Joe broke up with me, so I had to move back home with my parents. As devastated as I was, I knew I had to be strong for the tiny human growing in my belly.

I stopped being strong when I woke up nine weeks later to blood-stained sheets.

Nothing made sense. Nothing was right. No Joe. No baby. All the things I'd ever wanted were gone.

So, when my boss asked me what I wanted this morning, it was no surprise I didn't have an answer.

It was a normal morning. At least, it *was* before Joe walked into my office.

I thought it'd be easier after not seeing him for two months. But my heart strains against my chest like it's physically reaching out for him between the bars of its cage.

"How are you feeling?" he asks, shoving his hands into the pockets of his jeans. Tall and lean with blond hair and green eyes, I can't help but think how beautiful Joe's baby would've been.

"I'm fine."

"Your mom said you haven't been eating much lately."

My eyes snap up to his. "You've been talking to my mother?"

"When I heard what happened, I wanted to make sure you were all right."

A laugh escapes me. Here's a PSA to all the guys out there: When a girl laughs at something that clearly isn't funny, something's wrong. There's no turning back after that. You should probably run.

I roll my chair back and stalk around my desk to stand in front of him. "Why don't you go ask Brianna how she's doing?"

He winces. "That's not fair."

"Not fair? You of all people don't get to tell me what's fair."

Joe reaches for me, but I back away as if his hand is a disgusting slug. "Come on, Carla. Can't you find it in your heart to forgive me? I want to work things out."

My eyeballs almost pop out of my head. "So, now that our baby is *dead*, you want to work things out?"

Joe's mouth falls open. I'm not one for outbursts, in private or public. But I'm past caring. I lost more than the baby when I miscarried. Something inside me snapped.

Mr. Andrews, my boss, appears in the doorway. "Miss Evans, is everything okay?"

For the past two months, many people had asked me that very question. I'd always answered with the same forced smile and mechanical response.

Today, I swallow and say, "No. Everything is *not* okay."

He turns to Joe and sighs. "Why are you here, Mr. McKinney? What do you want?"

Joe's beautiful, emerald eyes lock with mine. "I want to work things out. I want to be together again."

My heart clenches and I scold it. Back in your cell, inmate.

"And what do you want, Miss Evans?"

What do I want?

I feel disoriented. I'm blinking like I've been woken up by a bucket of ice water. Flashes of my old life play on a reel in my mind.

I want what I once had.

I want what I lost.

But I can't go back to the way things were before I'd gotten pregnant. Nothing would be the same ever again. I had a plan then. Now, I'd have to make a new plan—a new life. One without Joe. One tinged with sadness over a baby who never got to be.

What do I want?

For the first time in my life, I don't know.

Maybe it's Joe's unexpected presence. Maybe it's the lack of food. Maybe it's the loss of control that sends me spiraling. Regardless of what caused it, I fall down a rabbit hole.

The words form on my tongue before the actual thought does. "I quit."

A deep crease forms between Mr. Andrews's eyebrows. "What?"

I lift my chin and square my shoulders. "I quit." And with that, I spin on my heels and swipe my purse off my desk. I pass the dumbfounded men, leave the office, and walk right out of the building. I pull out of the parking lot and into my parents' driveway ten minutes later.

Dodging the minefield of sports equipment and action figures, I stomp across the lawn and let myself in the house. When I reach my bedroom, I dump my toiletries and phone charger into the already-packed suitcase at the foot of my bed and zipper it shut. My yoga mat gets rolled up and tucked under my arm. I'm supposed to leave for New York tomorrow, but it looks like I'm getting a head start.

I scribble a quick note to my parents and leave it on the kitchen counter. *Decided to leave a day early. I'll call you along the way. Love you.*

Then I'm hoisting my suitcase into the back seat of my 1970 glossy black Camaro and backing out of the driveway.

I don't stop to think. I don't stop to call my best friend, Charlotte, who's the reason I'm driving all the way from Florida to New York in the first place. I don't even turn on the radio. I don't do anything except drive.

Thoughts don't start materializing until about an hour into my trip. This is when I realize I'd left in such a rush, I forgot to pack my flat iron. This is also when I realize I'm still wearing my work clothes: navy pencil skirt, white button-up blouse, and white espadrilles. Not exactly road trip attire.

When I started college last year, I'd gotten a job as an administrative assistant at the campus registrar's office. Secretarial work is pretty mundane, but Dad was happy to pull some strings with his friend, Mr. Andrews. It was one of the few campus jobs that went through the summer and worked perfectly around my class schedule.

And I'd just quit like an impulsive idiot.

Acid churns in my stomach as I think about how I didn't think at all. Before today, I was a planner. A thinker. I didn't make any decisions without thinking through a pros and cons list first. Walking out of my job, I hadn't thought about it for more than a millisecond. So, why did I do it? I'd walked out of my life as if I'd never return to it.

Maybe I don't want to.

I turn the radio on to help calm my nerves. Lisa Loeb sings, "Stay," and I crank it up as high as I can. Though I'm only half sure what the song is about, I belt it out with as much feeling as if I'd lived the lyrics myself. Lisa blends into Alanis, who turns into Stevie, and before I know it, I'm rocking out to Joan Jett.

Hours pass as I cruise up the East Coast. I stop for gas, load up on snacks, and get back on the road.

The farther I get from home, the better I feel. Calmer. Somewhere in North Carolina, I even smile. Dad said I should've flown because *"it's a brutal ride."* The flight from Florida to New York would've been a short couple of hours, but the idea of a solo road trip was too enticing to pass up. I'd wanted the time to myself to process and think. It felt like a rite of passage. There's nothing like freedom on the open road.

I guess my smile was a little too smug because the AC in my car picks this exact moment to crap out on me. This is the downside of driving a classic car. I wind down both windows, hoping the cross breeze will suffice in the August heat. The air is thick and sweat seeps into every possible crevice of my body, bringing doubt along with it.

Maybe Dad was right. Maybe this was a dumb idea. Maybe I should turn around.

My knuckles are white on the steering wheel again, so I take another deep breath. "What worries you, masters you."

As much as I love that quote from John Locke, I doubt he knew what it felt like to leave a flat iron behind in ninety percent humidity.

As if things aren't bad enough, my phone buzzes in the passenger seat. I groan before answering.

"Hi, Mom."

"Carla! Are you alright? Where are you?"

"I'm fine. I'm on the way to see Charlotte."

"I just spoke to Joe. He said you quit your job. What happened?"

"Why are you talking to Joe?"

"He wants to get back with you. Isn't that a good thing? I thought that's what you wanted."

"Why would I want to get back with him after he left me when I was pregnant with his child?"

She sighs as if I'm the exasperating one. "Carla, he made a mistake. He's young. You both are. He wants to make up for it. Maybe you should think about giving him another chance."

I bite my tongue so hard I'm surprised I don't taste blood. "You know what? I'm driving. I shouldn't be talking on the phone. I'll text you when I get to Charlotte's place."

I end the call and toss my phone onto the seat beside me. My eyes sting and the lines in the road before me blur together. Something must've gotten in my eyes. It's probably dust or pollen. A pebble probably ricocheted inside my car. I signal and pull onto the shoulder as my eyes continue to water.

I'm not a crier. Tears never fix anything, so I don't see the point. I didn't even cry when I had the miscarriage. Mom said I was in shock.

Maybe it's wearing off now, because the girl who just impulsively quit her job is now pulled over somewhere on I-95 crying her eyes out.

Chapter Two

THE PAST

DID YOU KNOW A CHILD IS PLACED INTO FOSTER CARE EVERY TWO minutes? There are 1,440 minutes in a day, so you can figure out how many kids per day that equals. It's a lot.

Of those kids, about half will drop out of high school. A fifth of them will even end up homeless. The statistics are grim. It's no wonder Cheryl, my case manager, hasn't told me any of this. I can't even be mad at her. I wouldn't know how to tell me if I were her. Could you look into a kid's eyes and tell him he'll never amount to anything in life? That the journey he's about to embark on will be difficult, and full of sorrow. That he'll never know what it feels like to be loved again.

I'm not being negative here. It's the truth. Mom was the only person who loved me, and even she didn't love me enough as she should've. If she did, she wouldn't be dead and I wouldn't be here, sitting on a stained couch in some stranger's living room listening to her tell me about how thrilled she is to be a foster parent. Spoiler alert: The only thing she's thrilled about is the money that comes attached to me.

This is the third home I've been to. Apparently I "wasn't the right fit" for the first two we'd visited. What they really meant was that I wasn't worth the money. I'm what's considered a "special case," and I don't mean orphan Annie special. I'm a traumatized fourteen-year old suffering with PTSD. Plus, I can't sing or tap dance.

Society somehow managed to glamorize foster care. Everyone imagines an infant being left at a fire house, and magically getting adopted by the quintessential happy couple who lives in a two-story house surrounded by a white picket fence. And maybe that does happen for some kids. *Lucky bastards*. No one knows how bad it is on the other side of that coin. Not even good old Cheryl here. She gets to clock out at the end of her day and go home to eat a hot meal.

No, the only people who know what it's really like to be a foster kid are the foster kids. We're supposed to be grateful for the roof over our heads, even though that roof drips onto your bed every time it rains. We're supposed to show appreciation for the food in our bellies, but that food is often stale or moldy. We're supposed to respect our foster parents despite the fact that respect should be earned, and let's face it —nobody ever respects someone who beats on them.

I'm not surprised by the statistics for kids like me.

"Thank you, Cheryl. It was nice seeing you again." My new foster mother, Debbie, smiles at me. "Thomas is going to be a great addition to our little family."

Part of me wants to drop to my knees and beg Cheryl to take me home with her. The other part of me knows better.

Once the door closes, Debbie's façade vanishes. She breezes past me without a second glance and collapses onto the couch, lighting up a cigarette before switching on the TV.

"Uh, excuse me, Miss Debbie?" I hate how pathetic my voice sounds right now, but I have to be cautious and feel this one out.

"What?"

"I'm really hungry."

"What do I look like, a chef? Get out of the way. You're blocking Judge Judy."

I shuffle around until I find the kitchen. I swing open each cabinet, hoping to find something edible. At the end of my search, I settle for a box of stale Cheerios and a tub of expired peanut butter. Don't knock it till you try it. Peanut butter is protein, and it makes the cereal taste a little less like cardboard. I scrape the green fuzz off the top layer of the tub before diving in. Expired food won't kill me. The most I'll get is an upset stomach. And don't they make penicillin out of mold? I heard that somewhere.

My body jolts when a brown ball of fur scampers across the floor. "You won't find much in here, buddy." I coat a few cereal pieces with peanut butter and place them on the floor. I'd always wanted a dog, but Mom said it would only be one more thing for Dad to hurt. In hindsight, I'm glad we never got one.

The mouse is quick to pounce on the cereal and sniffs the air for more.

"I bet you've eaten better meals out of a garbage, haven't you?"

I haven't resorted to dumpster diving yet. There were a few times over the past few months I'd been tempted. It's amazing how much food people waste. I'm in the stage where I'll stoop low enough to scrape mold off my food, but I'm not ready for half-eaten trash.

Funny how we all cling to our last shreds of dignity, like it makes a difference.

But it doesn't. Not when you're a statistic. Some people are destined for greatness. Others ... we're not destined for anything.

"Don't feed that filthy animal!" Debbie's screeching voice startles me. "What's wrong with you, boy?" She's quick to grab a broom, and swats at the mouse.

"Stop!" I grip the broomstick and attempt to yank it out of her hands. "Don't hurt it!"

"Get out of my way! These pests eat your food and shit all over the place." She shoves me into the wall, giving the mouse enough time to run for his life.

For a second, I think he'll get away. Then Debbie corners him and the broom crashes down on his little body. Three times she smashes it, until it's lifeless and bloodied.

I don't turn my head in time. I see everything. Maybe that's my destiny, to see all of the horrible things in this world.

"Why would you kill him? Why would you do that?" My knees hit the tile as I sob into my trembling hands.

Debbie tosses the broom onto the floor beside me. "That's the circle of life. Now get rid of him."

The image of that innocent mouse being killed will haunt my dreams long after I've moved on from Debbie's house.

It'll join the nightmares I have about Mom.

Welcome to the club.

Chapter Three

THE PRESENT

 arla

I DOUBLE-CHECK THE DIRECTIONS ON MY PHONE AND TURN ONTO the next street. The GPS shows two minutes remaining. I cannot wait to get out of this car and stretch. A cold beer would be nice too.

A flash of light reflects off my rear-view mirror. *Did someone just high-beam me?* I glance in the mirror and the red Dodge pick-up behind me flashes its lights again, this time accompanied by a blaring horn.

Crazy New York drivers. The speed limit is 25mph but he's all over me. So I do what any normal person would do. My foot eases off the gas. My speedometer now reads 10mph. "How's that, asshole?"

And there's the horn again.

The hotel comes into view. I signal and wait for the oncoming traffic to pass. I'm in the middle of making a left turn when the psycho behind me whips around me—on my left—causing me to slam on the brakes so I don't crash into him.

"Are you crazy?" I scream out my window. Who passes someone on the driver's side when she's trying to turn? Is this really how people on Staten Island drive?

His truck is lifted so high I can't see his face. "Learn how to drive!" he shouts.

"Good luck with your small penis, you overcompensating douchebag!"

He speeds away, massive tires kicking dust and gravel into the air.

I whip into the lot, park, and shut the engine. Loosening my grip on the steering wheel, I try to slow my breaths and calm down.

Welcome to Staten Island.

After I check in at the front desk, I ask the clerk to point me toward the nearest bar.

————

"I'll take a Corona, please."

I hand the bartender my fake ID and settle against the back of my stool. She pops the top off the bottle and slides it my way. I take a long swig.

"You don't strike me as the beer type."

I hold my hand up without looking at who the deep voice belongs to. "Save your energy for someone else, please." *Can't a girl sit alone at a bar without being hit on?*

"It doesn't really take much energy to have a conversation, but thanks for your concern."

I roll my eyes and take another few gulps of my beer. I pretend to watch the TV above the bar, though I can feel the stranger's eyes on me.

"Who are you rooting for?" he asks.

"What?"

"The fight you're staring at so intently. Who are you rooting for?"

"I'm not rooting for anyone. MMA is a barbaric sport. How these guys get paid mega bucks to beat each other up is beyond me. Just another testament to our Neanderthal society."

"Those guys aren't just beating each other up."

I gesture toward the screen. "Those two dudes are throwing punches at each other. That guy is bleeding profusely from his nose. They certainly aren't doing ballet."

The stranger chuckles. "Okay, so they are fighting. But there's more to it than that. It takes skill and training to do what they do."

"Oh, look. Now they're on the ground. That guy's going to lay on top of the other one for the next five minutes. You're right. Looks like they've had a lot of training." I drain the rest of my beer and stand. So much for enjoying a drink *alone*.

"You should stay and watch the fight. I'll prove to you just how much skill these guys have."

I spin around to face the annoying stranger, allowing myself to look at him for the first time.

Holy muscles.

I clamp my mouth shut to keep it from falling wide open. Brawny. Strapping. Muscular. Built. None of the words coming to mind seem adequate enough to describe the Herculean god sitting before me. It's almost a sin he covered himself up with all those tattoos. *Almost.* The intricate pieces of art twist around his muscular arms, all the way down to his knuckles. A tease of ink pokes out of the neckline of his shirt, stopping halfway up his neck. Every inch of his body has trouble written all over it.

His face though ... his face is a different story. It's so handsome it looks like it doesn't belong on his body. The icy-blue of his eyes is warmed by his smile, which is complete with a set of dimples. A backwards baseball cap covers his hair, but his thick brows and scruff peppering his chiseled jawline are as dark as a cup of coffee.

He's an oxymoron. The face of an angel with the body of Satan himself. A dark ray of light. A friendly nemesis. The man is menacingly beautiful.

And I'm gawking. I clear my throat and try to remember what it was he'd asked me. "I've had a long trip. I'm going to call it a night."

"Where you coming from?"

"Florida. Just arrived."

"And the first place you come to is a bar?"

My eyes narrow and I prop my hand on my hip. "Don't judge me. You don't know a thing about me."

His hands shoot up. "Hey, I wasn't judging. I was just making an observation."

"Well, don't do that either."

I turn to leave, but I'm stopped by his large, tattooed hand around my arm. It's a warm, gentle touch, and my skin sizzles. I yank my arm away, angry at my body for having such a reaction to this man.

"I'm sorry," he says. "I didn't mean to offend you. Sit. Let me buy you another beer."

"You don't have to do that."

He's waving the bartender over before I can stop him. "Corona for my friend ..." He looks at me expectantly.

"I'm not your friend."

He grins. "Corona for my not-a-friend."

His smile is so warm and inviting. It doesn't go with anything else on him. He looks unlike anyone I've ever seen. Or maybe he doesn't, and I'd just been too preoccupied to notice anyone else. Being in love is what I now refer to as *preoccupied*. It hurts less when I say it that way.

I'd been preoccupied with someone.

I'd been preoccupied with planning our future.

I'd been preoccupied with naming our unborn baby.

Now, I'm just preoccupied and alone.

That thought makes me want another beer, so I reclaim my stool. The bartender replaces my empty bottle with a new one and I tap it against the stranger's glass. "Cheers."

"So, how long are you here for?" he asks.

"A week."

"Are you visiting family?"

"Nope."

"Are you going to continue to give me one-word answers for the rest of the night?"

"Probably."

He smirks and returns his attention to the fight.

I tip my bottle toward his full glass of what looks like whiskey. "You haven't touched your drink."

"Wow. That was a whole five words."

One corner of my mouth turns up, but I stop it before it goes any further. This guy doesn't need any encouragement.

"I'm TJ by the way."

I shake his extended hand. "Nice to meet you."

"You're seriously not going to tell me your name?"

"You're seriously going to make me watch this fight?"

"You seem convinced of this notion that fighting doesn't take skill. As a fighter, I feel compelled to convince you otherwise."

"Ah, you're a fighter. That explains the muscles."

"You're checking out my muscles?"

"I'm not checking them out. I'm just ... making an observation."

TJ chuckles and I steal another glance at him out of the corner of my eye. Those dimples should be illegal. His entire body should be illegal, really. He even has long, dark lashes that frame those striking eyes. It almost hurts to look directly at him. A muscular eclipse.

He points to the screen. "Watch this guy's next move."

I tear my eyes off TJ and watch as the man on TV with the bloody nose twists his legs around his opponent's arm. I cringe as the poor man's elbow is bent to its limit.

"Why doesn't he tap out already?"

"Because he's thinking of a way out." TJ's head whips to the left. "Wait. You know about tapping out?"

I nod, still waiting for the man to tap before his arm breaks.

"You've watched MMA fights before?"

"I had a boyfriend who was into this garbage."

He clutches his chest. "Words hurt, you know."

My lips twitch. "You said you wanted to prove me wrong." I cross my legs and tap my foot. "Let's hear it."

TJ swivels on his stool to face me, exposing his tattooed legs. "Any kind of fighting takes skill. It's more than size and throwing your fists around. It's more than how strong you are. Your mind needs to be sharp. You need to know your opponent, assess his skills, and calculate how you're going to counter those skills. You need to figure out your next attack while you're in the trenches taking fire.

"On the other hand, you can know all the technical moves in the world and still lose the fight. You need heart, too. You need the tenacity to stay and fight."

I might not be into fighting, but the way TJ talks about it is the most passionate I've heard anybody talk about anything in a long time. It makes me want to hear more. Or maybe I just want him to continue talking so I can keep staring at him.

"So what would you do if you were that guy on TV right now? Your opponent is on top of you. He's clearly stronger than you, and he's about to snap your arm like a twig. How do you get out of that?"

"Sometimes, you don't get out of it," TJ says. "One of the skills you need to have is the art of losing."

I raise my beer. "Now there's a skill we could all use."

"Oh, yeah? What've you lost?"

My stomach twists at the reminder. I take a few long swigs of beer instead of answering. One of *my* skills is the art of ignoring the things I don't want to talk about.

His eyebrows lift. "I've hit a nerve."

"To be fair, you've pretty much been standing on it this whole time."

TJ blinds me with another smile, and I allow my mouth to curve a little higher than before.

The few patrons inside the bar shout in unison. The guy whose arm was about to break manages to get out of his opponent's grip and begins pummeling his face. The referee stops the fight. The underdog wins.

"That," TJ says, leaning in closer, "takes skill."

My heart rate kicks up a notch as he lingers inches from my face. He smells clean and cologned, though he looks as if he should smell like whiskey and bad decisions.

I lean away from him because I'm pretty sure my deodorant stopped working somewhere around the sixth hour of my drive. The Taco Bell sweating through my pores probably isn't helping either.

"How come you're not fighting on TV?" I ask.

"I'd rather help other fighters make their way."

"Is that what you do?"

"I own a gym. I train people who need me."

"You don't want the fame and fortune?"

TJ sloshes the liquid around in his glass. "That life doesn't interest me."

"What interests you?"

"Lots of things."

"Like?"

"Sexy travelers dressed like secretaries."

My heart squeezes and I reprimand myself for it. "Like I said before: Save your energy for someone else."

"I bet you're a secretary."

"I was before I got here."

"Why'd you quit?"

The million dollar question. "I ... I don't know."

"Was your boss an asshole?"

"Not at all."

"Then what?" TJ's head tilts, appraising me while he waits for my answer. When I don't have one, he signals for the waitress. "Can I see a menu, love?"

The waitress blushes as she twirls her long ponytail around her manicured finger. "You always order the same thing. Why do you even bother with the menu?"

"I like to keep you on your toes. Maybe one day I'll change it up and surprise you."

She giggles. "Cheeseburger with fries, then?"

TJ nods. "You hungry, my not-a-friend?"

I hadn't planned on staying for dinner, but a meal outside a drive-thru sounds enticing right about now. "I'll have what he's having. Well-done, please."

TJ quirks a brow. "You like eating hockey pucks?"

"You like your burgers still mooing on the plate?"

There's that cocky smirk again. "Why don't you tell me your name, since we're about to have dinner together."

I hold up my index finger. "We are not having dinner together. We're having dinner ... simultaneously."

"What if I guess it? Will you tell me?"

"The odds of you guessing my name are highly unlikely."

"I'll take my chances." TJ squares his shoulders. "Jessica."

"Nope."

"Rebecca."

"No."

"Michelle."

I shake my head.

"Is it a southern name, like Sara Lee? Or one of those fancy millennial names, like McKenzie?"

"I'm not giving you any hints."

"There's a billion names to choose from. Narrow it down for me, at least."

"Knowing my name won't make a difference."

"Of course it will. I'd be able to put a name to that beautiful face of yours."

"Still won't matter."

"Maybe you have a name that matches your uptight personality. Barbara? Josephine?"

My skin heats. "I am not uptight! Again, you don't even know me."

"Just making another observation." TJ makes a show of surveying my body from head to toe. "That outfit couldn't have been comfortable driving all those hours in."

"Let me guess: You're going to feed me a line about how my outfit would look better on your bedroom floor."

"See? I knew you were uptight. Who says we have to have sex in my bedroom?"

I roll my eyes. *This is why he's so hot. He has to be, with such an irritating personality.*

When the waitress places our plates in front of us, I scarf my burger down in silence, order a third beer, and polish off my fries. Either I'm starving, or my best friend was right when she told me New York food is way better than the food in Florida.

TJ pushes his plate toward me. "Want the rest of my fries?"

"You're not going to finish them?"

"You look hungry and I'm a little scared. You attacked that burger like a scene from Animal Planet."

My smile breaks through and I duck behind the thick curtain of my hair.

"Hey, don't hide that smile. I've been waiting to see if it would show."

Honestly, I was waiting for it too.

"It looks good on you. You should smile more often."

"I used to."

TJ stretches his arms out on either side of him, resting one on the back of my chair. "And does that have something to do with your MMA-watching ex-boyfriend?"

"Do you always ask this many personal questions to people you don't know?"

"People find it easier to open up to a stranger. It's like going to confession. You lay out all your sins and feel better when you're done."

"You don't feel better because it's a stranger. You feel better because you believe the priest absolves you of your sins. Huge difference."

"Why don't you ask me something, then? I'll tell you a secret."

I set my empty beer bottle on the bar. "Fine. Why order a glass of whiskey if you're not going to drink it?"

"I used to be an alcoholic." TJ shrugs like it's no big deal. "I come here to celebrate what I've overcome."

"Or you just like to torture yourself."

Though he doesn't respond, TJ's eyes meet mine and tell me I'm right. In their glacial depths, pain reflects back at me.

My stomach clenches. "Why are you punishing yourself?"

"I guess I like the pain. It's a reminder that I'm still here ... in the fight."

"Do you use fighting metaphors for everything in life? I bet you quote Rocky on the regular." I drop my forehead into my palm and groan. "You have *Eye of the Tiger* as your ringtone, don't you?"

"Alright, smartass. My turn, and you have to answer. What's your story? Why are you in New York?"

"No story. Just here to visit my best friend."

His eyebrows lift, prompting me for more.

I sigh. "My best friend moved here after she graduated high school. I haven't seen her in a while and I miss her."

"So why aren't you with her right now?"

"She thinks I'm arriving tomorrow."

"And she thinks this because ..."

"Because that's what I told her."

"Why are you here now?"

I breathe in and out several times, picking apart the crumpled napkin in my plate. I haven't talked to anyone about this. Maybe TJ's right. Maybe opening up to someone, anyone, would make me feel better. Besides, it's not like I'd ever have to see him again.

"My ex and I were together for four years. We were engaged. Everything was going according to plan. Then I got pregnant. We were careful, you know. I was on the pill, but they always warn you about that small possibility. Joe didn't want me to keep the baby, but I couldn't kill it. I couldn't just pretend like it never happened. So he broke up with me."

"You're pregnant?" TJ asks, his eyes darting from my empty beer bottle to my stomach. "You know that could hurt the baby."

I shake my head and tell him, "There is no baby."

TJ's eyebrows collapse. "What do you mean?"

"I had a miscarriage." I shrug, trying to seem as nonchalant about my devastation as TJ was about his addiction. "I lost everything."

"You didn't lose *everything*. Plan A didn't work out, so now you move on to Plan B."

"I don't have a Plan B."

"As long as you're alive, you'll always have a Plan B."

"What if I don't like Plan B?"

"Plan A wasn't meant to be. You've got to let it go."

I let go of Joe. My uterus let go of the egg. I let go of my job. I pretty much let go of my sanity. I've let go of so much, I could change my name to Elsa. An ice fortress of solitude does sound enticing right now.

I signal for the bartender. "You know, I used to believe in things being meant to be. Now I realize it's just a way to comfort ourselves. When something doesn't go our way, we claim it wasn't meant to be and that helps us cope. Maybe bad things just happen. Maybe there isn't a reason for any of it."

"Does it matter if there's a reason? The bad shit still happens either way."

I nod as I pull out my wallet to pay my tab.

TJ intercepts and slips the bartender his card. "Dinner's on me."

"Oh, no. No. That's really not necessary. You don't have to do that." I reach over the bar to hand the bartender my cash, but she winks and walks away with TJ's card.

So much for solidarity, sister.

I stand and smooth out my skirt. "Thank you. You didn't have to do that."

"I wanted to," TJ says, signing the credit card slip. "It was a pleasure meeting you ... Sarah?"

"Still no."

He walks out with me into the parking lot. "Do you need a ride?"

"I've got my own."

TJ stops beside his vehicle and swings the door open.

My eyes go wide. "It was you!"

"What was me?"

I wave my hand at his truck. "The douchebag in the red truck who cut me off before I got here. It was you."

TJ's head falls back as he barks out a laugh. "You're the one who told me I was overcompensating for my little dick?"

"I called it a small penis, for the record."

One thick brow arches. "Don't I get a chance to set the record straight?"

"Let the record show he drives a red, lifted truck." I point to his tires. "With rims. Seems like an open-and-shut case to me."

"Tough jury."

I shake my head, raking my eyes over him. "It's surprising, someone of your size having a small penis."

TJ steps into my personal space until he's so close I have to crane my neck to look at him. "Oh, it's surprising. Just not in the way you think."

Energy pulses at my veins with his large frame towering over me, but I don't budge. I can't. TJ's intense gaze pins me to the ground. I'm an ant under his magnifying glass, and all I can do is burn.

"When's the last time you did something spontaneous?" he asks. "Something you didn't plan. Something you didn't see coming."

"I just quit my job."

"Before that."

Never. I hike a shoulder. "I don't know."

"And how did that feel, walking out without a plan?" His fingers trail up my arms, leaving goosebumps in their wake.

My chest heaves with ragged breaths. "Scary."

"And?" He drags his knuckles along my neck.

My throat's dry, voice a whisper. "Freeing."

"Getting warmer." His thumb strums my bottom lip.

Every cell in my body screams, drawing me closer to him. "It was ... exhilarating."

"There she is." His tongue slips out and wets his lips, like a hungry wolf who's about to devour his prey. "It's good to feel like that once in a while. Don't you agree?"

I shake my head, then I nod. I have no idea what he's asking anymore. All I can concentrate on is his massive presence, his touch, those velvety lips. He's scrambling my brain.

Without asking, TJ covers my mouth with his. His lips are so plush and warm, I melt against them. He tugs my hair as his tongue slides out, begging for entrance. I should push him off me. Instead, I open for him, eager and willing. The kiss is slow, full of passion, and I feel it all the way down to my toes. I can say with absolute conviction: I've never been kissed like this before.

TJ exudes such confidence and it feels like it's all transferring to me. Like in this moment, I've become someone else. Maybe it's the alcohol, or maybe I left the old me back in Florida. Either way, I can't seem to care that I'm kissing a stranger in a parking lot outside a bar called *Big Nose Kate's.*

One night. I just want one night.

I want to forget.

I want to be free.

I want to let go.

That's why, when TJ asks me if I want to go back to his place, I say *yes.*

J

"Where do you think you're going?"

"Out." I don't look in Dave's direction as I stride toward the door.

"Out where? I didn't hear you ask permission to leave. Did you hear anything, Arlene?"

Arlene's nose glides across the coffee table. "Why do you care where he's going?" she asks, wiping the remnants of the powder from her nostrils.

"Because this is *my* house, bitch." Dave pounds his fist into his chest as he stands. Apparently, this gesture is supposed to make men look tough instead of the dumb pricks they really are. *Thanks for that one, Denzel.*

"This isn't a house. It's an apartment." I shouldn't have said that, I know. But the guy's a moron. I can't help myself.

"Don't get smart with me, you little shit." Dave waddles over to where I'm standing. "Go to your room."

"I said I'm going out." I yank open the door.

Dave's hand grips the back of my neck. "And I said go to your room."

"Why can't you just leave me alone? Go get high and fuck your crack-whore wife."

Dave lurches and his fist connects with my right eye. I fall onto my back, throwing my arms over my face.

"You never learn, do you?" His boot sinks into my ribcage that's still sore from yesterday's beating.

Sometimes Arlene tries to stop Dave from hitting me, but she's too high to care right now.

I should be crying from the pain, but all I can do is laugh. Provoking Dave fuels me. "Are you winded already? You should really lay off the Twinkies."

Dave balls my shirt in his fists, lifts me up, and slams my back against the wall. We're nose to nose, the odor emitting from his greasy skin mixing with the stench of his breath. His unkempt beard holds onto remnants of his lunch.

"You don't talk to me like that. I'm in charge here. I put the roof over your head. You do what I say. You got that?"

I wave my hand in front of my nose. "You should take some of that money and go see a dentist. Your mouth smells like gum disease."

He pops me in the jaw and pummels my stomach, again and again. I take it and wait 'til it's over. Dave is obese. He tuckers out quicker than most.

Most high schoolers play a sport or an instrument. Maybe they have dinner with their families, or see a movie with friends. For me? A kick to the gut and a few punches to the head is a typical Friday night.

Dave isn't the first monster I've encountered. I've endured worse. In the past year, I've met several different kinds of monsters. Dave doesn't scare me.

Nothing does.

Fear doesn't control me anymore.

———

"WHO GAVE YOU THAT SHINER?" WOODS ASKS.

I look down at his shoes. Shiny as always.

"Look at me, Thomas."

"I told you not to call me that anymore."

Woods sighs. "Who gave you that shiner?"

"Why do you ask questions you already know the answer to?"

"I can't help you if you don't tell me what's going on."

"You couldn't help me even if you knew." I dip three French fries into a glob of ketchup and shove them into my mouth. McDonald's tastes as good as Mom's home-cooked meals when you haven't eaten all day.

"Is it someone at school? Are you being bullied?"

I glare at him before taking a bite of my cheeseburger. *As if I'd let another kid do this to me.*

"Then who? Because if it's your foster parent, you can come down to the station with me and file a report. Or I can come with you to social services and you can tell someone there."

"What's the point?"

"The point? You'd be placed in another home where you don't get beat."

"Another home. Great." I give Woods a thumbs-up and go back to eating.

"I know you've been bounced around a lot this year, but you can keep trying until you find the right home."

"Don't you get it? There isn't going to be a right home for me. Nice, loving couples don't want to adopt a troubled fifteen-year old. Just ask your wife."

His jaw works under his skin. "That's not fair. You know I'd take you in if I could."

Woods was the police officer to arrive at my house every time I'd call when I was growing up. He'd let me sit in the front seat of his car and turn on the lights and sirens while Mom got checked by the paramedic. A few years ago, Woods made detective. Still, he was always there for me whenever I called for help. He's the only friend I have.

I busy my mouth with chewing instead of saying the words I'm holding inside. I know it's not his fault I'm in this situation, and I can't blame his wife for not allowing him to adopt me. She'd probably give him hell if she knew he was still meeting me after his shift every Friday night.

But there's nowhere for my pain to go. Anger erupts and pours over me, blanketing the hurt. I succumb to the rage. It's easier that way. The anger comforts me.

So, Woods will sit here and pretend like he can fix my problems.

I'll sit here and pretend like everything isn't as bad as it is.

We both know the truth.

"Are they feeding you at least?"

I shake my head. "Do you mind if I order another cheeseburger to go?"

"Order whatever you want." He hands me a twenty and stands. "I've got to head out."

"I know."

"I'm serious about talking to social services. I'll go there with you and we can sort this out."

"It's fine. Don't worry about me." Nobody else does.

Woods lifts my chin toward the light, examining my black eye. "Only four more years until you're legal. Things will get better for you. You'll see."

Only four. "Yeah. See you next week."

He reaches into a shopping bag and pulls out a black North Face jacket. "You'll need something warm for the winter. Happy Birthday, Thomas."

I cringe at the reminder. I dread my birthday, but not in the way most people do because they don't want to turn another year older. My birthday marks the day I watched my mother die. There's nothing happy or exciting about it.

Happy Birthday? What a joke.

arla

I'M IN A STRANGER'S BATHROOM.

Correction: I just freshened up with half a dozen baby wipes in a stranger's bathroom because I'm about to have sex with said stranger.

I check the time on my phone. I've already been in here for seven minutes. I have to exit this bathroom soon, otherwise he's going to think I have a stomachache. With my hand on the doorknob, I inhale a deep breath through my nose and blow it out my lips. My heart pounds with every step I take into the living room.

TJ's apartment is very plain, though it's a decent size for being above the gym he owns. Bare, white walls, a brown leather couch facing a flat screen, and a rustic coffee table are all that fill the room I'm standing in.

Marie Kondo would be proud, though it makes me wonder what, if anything, sparks joy in TJ.

TJ emerges from the kitchen and hands me a water bottle. "Sorry. I don't keep alcohol here."

"Water is fine." Any more than the three beers I've already had and

I'd be sloppy. I need to keep my wits about me, even if I'm doing something as witless as this. I twist the cap off and chug half the bottle.

"You seem nervous," he says.

I do this weird, high-pitched laugh that I've never done before. "I'm not nervous."

TJ steps closer, reaching out to twirl a strand of my hair around his finger. "Why did you come here?" The way he's looking at me halts the excuse on my tongue, eyes boring into mine as if they already know the truth.

"I guess I just want to forget ... about everything."

"To forget about him."

"Is it bad if I say yes?"

"There's nothing wrong with that. We all have someone we're trying to forget."

It's the way he says it. It's in his voice, the forlorn look in his eyes. Like he's hurting the same as me. My heart aches and I wonder what he might've endured.

Wait. Why do I feel bad for him? I don't even know this guy. For all I know, he could be a jerk. It's always the ones who seem nice and make you trust them before they rip your heart out.

Come to think of it, he was sitting alone in the bar. There aren't any pictures of family members hanging on his walls. My stomach drops as I realize I'm in a stranger's apartment and no one even knows I'm here. I could be in danger.

I take a step back. "Uh ... are you a serial killer or something?"

TJ's eyebrows dip. "What?"

"I just realized I don't know you. You're a stranger." I continue taking small steps away from him. "You could be some crazed murderer or something. You don't have any pictures on your walls." I take another step back and bang my ankle on the leg of the coffee table. *Crap.* This is how it happens. The girl always gets hurt or falls right before the killer closes in on her.

TJ's grinning. It's not an evil *I'm going to kill you now* grin, but more like an *I'm laughing at you because you're acting ridiculous* grin. "For the record, if you're trying to escape, you shouldn't back yourself into a corner. It's pretty much the first rule of survival."

I glance over my shoulder. Yup, I'm in a corner. "Maybe I have a plan you don't know about. Maybe I know karate."

"If you can do karate, then I can do ballet."

I chew on my bottom lip. "I'd like to see you do ballet."

TJ advances toward me. "Oh, I've got moves. They might not be ballet moves, but I've got 'em."

Pricks of apprehension sting my mind as I'm reminded why I'm here. "Are you going to show me your moves?"

"If you'll let me near you." He continues inching closer and my shoulder blades hit the wall. He tilts my chin with his finger until I'm looking into his eyes. "I'm not going to make you do anything you don't want to do, but I can assure you: You're going to want me to do all the things I'm going to do to you."

Every bone in my body turns to Jell-O. The reservations I had going in to this evaporate into the air. His confidence is intoxicating and it courses through me, stripping me of my inhibitions.

"For the record," I whisper, "I had an escape plan."

TJ leans in so his lips brush against mine as he speaks. "For the record, I don't have *Eye of the Tiger* as my ringtone."

"For the record, I don't believe you."

He laughs, low and raspy, the sound reverberating inside me. He begins unbuttoning my blouse, slowly, without breaking eye contact.

My breaths are short, skin humming with the flick of each button. He opens my blouse and slips the chiffon down my arms. He unzips my skirt next and it falls at my feet.

I'm standing before a stranger in nothing but my plain cotton bra and panties. "I would've worn something sexier if I'd known I'd be having sex with a stranger tonight."

His eyes glide over every bare part of me. "You are an incredibly sexy woman, and it should be a man's privilege to see you like this."

Another wave of his confidence crashes over me. "Maybe I'd feel more comfortable if I wasn't the only one half-naked."

TJ lifts his T-shirt up and over his head, his baseball cap coming off with it.

And I'm dead.

I died.

TJ took off his shirt to reveal the most spectacularly carved set of abs I've ever seen. Elaborate tattoos span his chest and continue down each side of his ribcage, disappearing into the waistband of his shorts. His cubed abs are ink-free, which makes them stand out even more. I reach out to touch him, my fingers moving of their own volition to trace the artwork that continues along his skin.

"Wow," I say on an exhale.

"The ink or the muscles?"

"Both."

TJ's fingers push into my hair and give a gentle tug, sending shivers down my spine. I stretch up onto my toes, desperate to taste his mouth again. His tongue delves between my lips in search for mine. His kiss makes my knees buckle, and in one effortless swoop he lifts me up and carries me to his bedroom.

I land on his bed, the dark blue comforter puffing up around me. He pulls down his shorts. The open doorway casts just enough light into the room to allow me to see the white boxer briefs hugging his hips as he climbs onto the bed. Tattoos continue onto his thighs. My eyes can't decide where to look—the artwork on his skin, the bulging muscles in his arms as he crawls toward me, or the wicked look in his eyes.

Positioning himself above me, TJ cages me in with his arms. Our slow kisses become feverish with each passing second as he presses himself against me. He slips his hand between my back and the mattress to unhook my bra. I drop the straps and toss it onto the floor like the nuisance it is. Then his mouth is on my skin. He's taking his time kissing and licking every bare inch of me.

As if this isn't just a means to an end.

As if he's enjoying this.

As if there's nothing else he'd rather be doing.

This is new to me, this slow worshiping of my body.

When his lips kiss their way back to mine, his hand travels down my stomach and over my panties. My back arches as I exhale, body begging him to continue.

He slides his fingers under the thin cotton. "Is this what you want?"

"Yes." My voice is filled with need and desperation. *This is exactly what I want.*

"Then you need to tell me your name, baby girl."

My eyes pop open to meet his amused gaze. He has me in the palm of his hand. *Literally.* I fight the smile tugging at my lips and try to replace it with a scowl.

He chuckles and plants a kiss on my cheek, his fingers frozen inside my underwear.

I roll my hips against his hand. "You don't have to move. I can get there all by myself, you know."

"As hot as that would be, I can't allow it." TJ removes his hand, and I groan at the loss of his touch.

We are at a stalemate. I could lie. I could tell him another woman's name, but that idea doesn't sit right with me. I don't want to hear anyone else's name but mine on his lips. I need this.

"It's Carla."

TJ smiles as if I told him he won the lottery, those dimples twisting my insides. "Carla. I never would've guessed that."

"Told ya."

TJ's fingers return to me, and all conversation ends. He pays such close attention to every sound and movement I make, as if his only desire is to learn exactly what I need. Then he yanks my panties down, settles between my legs, and tastes me.

I want to tell him he doesn't have to do that but I can't seem to find the words, or maybe I don't want to find them. His attentiveness quells my worries, allowing me to take everything he's giving me like it's my right to have it.

Maybe it should be.

Maybe it is.

I reach down to thread my fingers through his hair and grip the back of his head, pushing myself against his tongue, needing more. He bends my legs up until my knees are pressed against my chest, and the feeling of being spread wide open for him nearly sends me rocketing off the bed.

My hand shoots up to cover my mouth on instinct, but TJ quickly uncovers it, holding my wrist down against the mattress. I'm glad, because this feels too good to keep inside. I've never moaned this loud before, but I've also never had anyone go down on me like this.

With Joe, foreplay was either rushed or skipped altogether. Sex was a one-man mission until he reached his release. Half the time, I never came unless it was caused by my own doing. It wasn't about me, or us, and I'd accepted that.

This is not the case with TJ. The way he's working his tongue on me is hot, wet ecstasy. The build of the slow burn between my thighs begins to mount. As if it's his cue, TJ slips a finger inside me. He curls it over and over again, beckoning for my orgasm to come to him while his tongue keeps the rhythm.

Something ignites within me, and it's more than just physical relief. There's a shift in my universe as I let go, surrendering myself mind, body and soul. I can't pinpoint what it means, but I know I want *more*.

As I come down from the mind-blowing orgasm and attempt to catch my breath, TJ crawls on top of me with a grin stretched wide across his face.

I fumble with the elastic on his boxers until he pushes them off. I peer down as he frees himself and my eyes go wide.

"What was that you said about a tiny penis?" he asks.

"I'm kind of surprised it's not covered in tattoos like the rest of you."

TJ chuckles as he reaches into his nightstand for a condom. Once he rolls it on, any trace of humor vanishes and is replaced with his heated gaze. He slides himself inside me, agonizingly slow, as if he wants to savor every drop of sensation it brings.

I wrap my legs around him and trace the tattoo on his neck with my tongue. When I bite his earlobe, he plunges all the way into me and groans. I dig my heels into his backside—yes, that's tattooed as well—and move my hips in sync with his.

He captures my lips and dips his tongue into my mouth, mirroring the motion of his thrusts. Everything is deliciously slow and controlled. But we can only endure this for so long.

TJ lifts my leg and hooks it over his shoulder. He pulls almost all the way out of me and pushes in again, diving deeper than before.

"Yes," I whisper, spurring him to give me more.

That cocky smirk ticks up at one side of his mouth. His length pulls out and I clench around him as he drives into me faster, again and again. My head is spinning, my body aching with need. I've never known that it could be like this. That sex could feel like this.

He tosses my other leg over his shoulder. His hands grip my hips so tightly, I'm sure I'll be left with bruises. There's something about his long, tattooed fingers holding onto me that fascinates me—fuels me.

I lift my arms and plant my hands on the headboard for leverage as I arch into TJ's thrusts.

"Fuck, Carla." His voice is a guttural sound, and the look he gives me is primal. "Come now. I need you to come again for me."

I surrender everything to him—my pain, my heartache—he takes it all. All that's left is pure, unleashed, pleasure. He waits for me and we come together. A moment of rapture at the will of a beautiful stranger.

TJ collapses onto the bed and curls me into him. Our staggered breaths fill the silence.

It's too soon to feel regret—not that I could regret something that felt *that* good. But now that our moment is over, uncertainty creeps back in. *What do I do now? Should I get up and leave? Am I staying the night?*

TJ wraps his giant arm around my midsection, as if he can sense my unease. "I'm warning you: I like to cuddle."

"The tattooed muscle head likes to cuddle?"

"He does. Will you stay?"

I shrug. "I don't know how these things work."

"They work however you want them to work. If you want to stay, you stay. If you want to leave, I'll walk you out."

Such a gentleman. "I bet you make all the girls swoon."

"Not all of them."

Who? I'd love to meet the woman who didn't fall at this guy's feet. I turn on my side to face him. "Earlier, you said we all have someone we're trying to forget. Who is she?"

"Someone I shouldn't have fallen in love with."

"Why shouldn't you have fallen in love with her?"

"Love isn't meant for me."

We're a pair, aren't we? Two broken hearts searching for relief. I sigh. "Def Leppard had it right."

"Love bites?"

"Nope. Love is like a bomb."

"Are you really taking love advice from a song that strippers dance to?"

"Shut up, I'm serious." Love is a bomb, obliterating everything and everyone in its vicinity. I roll onto my back and stare at the ceiling. "My ex is with someone else now, you know. Only took him two weeks after we broke up. Then he showed up at my job and said he wants to get back together."

"That's why you quit."

"I just got in my car, went home to get my suitcase, and drove here."

"In the secretary outfit."

"In the secretary outfit *that got me laid*."

TJ throws his head back and laughs. "Touché." He rolls out of bed and strides to the bedroom door. "I'm gonna grab us some more water."

I prop myself up on my elbows and watch him leave, taking in every inch of his glorious body. His broad shoulders and lats lead down in a V, dipping in at the small of his back. One muscular ass cheek is tattooed while the other is smooth and bare. I contemplate which one's my favorite.

Can't believe I just had sex with *that*.

My fingers trace my swollen lips. It's like I've been marked, every part of my body branded by TJ's touch.

Yesterday, I never would've done something like this.

Everything's different.

I feel different.

It began before I met TJ ... but after tonight, I'm certain that nothing will ever be the same again.

Chapter Six

THE PAST

J

CARS LINE THE STREET WHEN I ROUND THE CORNER. THE MUSIC gets louder as I get closer. The smell of weed gets stronger too. Another house party. *So much for sleeping tonight.*

My ninth foster home is my favorite. I use the term *favorite* loosely. It's like playing a game of *Would You Rather?* when both choices make you sick and you're stuck picking the lesser of two evils. I'm not getting hugs or home-cooked meals, but I'm not getting hit. And when you're a reject foster kid, that's saying something.

I opt for the back entrance. It allows me to come and go as I please. My bedroom is an unfinished basement that smells like a mixture of mold and bleach. It might be dingy, but I sleep on a futon. Again, it's the little things.

I lock the door behind me. My body stills when I notice someone sitting on my futon. "Get out."

"That's no way to treat a guest." The voice belongs to a female.

I flip on the lights. *Damn.* Long legs. Auburn hair. Creamy skin.

Full, pushed-up tits. She's definitely older than me, but by how much I can't tell. Either way, she's out of my league.

"Shouldn't you be enjoying the party upstairs?" I shrug off my jacket and toss it onto the floor.

"I'm having my own party down here." She gestures to the items spread out beside her: needle, elastic band, spoon, and lighter. "Want to join me?"

"What kind of party is this?" I've seen people smoke weed and snort cocaine, but I haven't been exposed to this.

"This is unlike anything you'll ever experience."

"How old are you?"

"Hasn't anyone ever taught you it's rude to ask a woman her age?"

I shrug and take a seat on the edge of the futon. "No one's taught me much of anything."

The woman tilts her head while she appraises me. "How old are *you*?"

"That depends on what time it is."

She glances at her watch. "Twelve-thirty."

"Then I'm sixteen."

Her eyebrows lift. "It's your birthday?"

"Yup."

"You're in luck, birthday boy. I've got the best gift for you." She leans over and ties a piece of elastic around my bicep.

I let her, because she smells nice and I've got a clear shot down her shirt while she's bending over like that.

She catches me looking. "Like what you see in there?"

I swallow and nod.

Leaning in another few inches, she brushes her lips against mine. "Have you ever had sex before?"

I shake my head. As if the tent in my pants isn't enough of an indication.

She undoes the elastic on my arm and straddles me instead. Her skirt rides up her thighs and I'm pretty sure she's not wearing any underwear. "Let's change that." She presses her lips to mine and grinds her hips against me.

I don't know how long a dude is supposed to last, this being my first encounter with a female and all, but I'm pretty close to busting in my pants.

She fumbles with my belt. I help by unbuttoning my jeans and pulling the zipper down, hoping she doesn't notice my shaking hands. She reaches into my boxers and pumps me a few times. Before I know what's happening, she pushes me inside herself.

My eyes go wide. "Don't we need protection or something?"

She throws her head back and laughs while she rides me. "I'm clean, birthday boy. Don't worry. And I can't get pregnant. My husband and I have been trying for years."

Husband? How old is this woman? That thought is quickly replaced by the intense pleasure mounting in my dick. She's so warm and wet. *God, this feels so*—and I just came.

The redhead laughs. I might not have experience, but I know laughter isn't a good thing after you've just finished having sex with someone.

"We'll go again," she says. "That was just the warm-up."

I do what she says and follow her lead. Put my hands here. Kiss her there. She teaches me what women like. I last longer the second time and manage to hold out until after she orgasms.

"How did that feel, birthday boy?"

"Amazing," I say in between breaths.

She re-ties the elastic around my arm. "Yeah, well ... an orgasm is going to seem like nothing after this."

I watch as she holds the spoon above the flame of the lighter. I watch as the powder liquefies. I watch as she sucks it up with the needle. I watch as she smiles.

Right before the needle punctures my vein, there's a voice screaming in my head. It's telling me to stop. It sounds a lot like Mom.

"What will this do to me?" I ask.

"It will make all the pain go away."

That's all I've ever wanted. *I'm sorry, Mom, but you're not here.*

I squeeze my eyes shut until the needle pulls out. While I'm waiting for something to happen, though I'm not sure what, the redhead injects herself with the needle.

At the many schools I'd been to, they'd always taught us about the dangers of using drugs. Sharing needles. Overdosing. Addiction. But no one ever tells us about how incredible drugs feel.

The rush of euphoria.

My arms and legs go limp. The memories that plague my mind day after day fade away into a haze.

I am in blissful oblivion.

And I never want to return.

Chapter Seven
THE PRESENT

arla

CHARLOTTE AND I HAVE BEEN FRIENDS SINCE WE WERE KIDS. WE grew up in the same small town and went to the same small school. We were always together, until Charlotte and her father disappeared.

Two nights after we'd danced the night away at prom, her father's bakery burned down. I went to her house the next morning, but she and her father were already gone. For an entire year, I didn't get one single call or text from her. I had no idea where they went, or what had happened. We went from inseparable best friends to complete radio silence.

Their bodies never showed up in the ashes, but I mourned them all the same.

A year later, right after I'd had the miscarriage, Charlotte called to tell me she was coming home. As elated as I was that she was okay, I couldn't help feeling angry that I'd spent twelve months being worried sick about her, wondering if she was even alive. I was also angry after having to go through the most difficult time in my life without my best friend.

To add insult to injury, Charlotte came back happier than ever, in love with a boy she'd met in New York. She had an amazing new life, while I was stuck in my crumbling old life.

Granted, Charlotte had been hunted down by Mafioso men who almost killed her, her father, and her new boyfriend. She didn't tell me where she was going because she didn't want to involve me in any way. Still, I hadn't rolled out the welcome wagon upon her arrival like I should've, and I needed to make up for that. Hence me driving up for a visit.

"Carla!" Charlotte squeals on the other end of the phone. "Are you on your way?"

"I'm already here. I'm in my hotel room as we speak." *Just did the walk of shame after my night of wild sex with a stranger.*

"You're in a hotel? I thought you were staying with me."

"I didn't want to cramp your style."

"Carla, I told you to stay with me and Dad."

"It's fine. I'm already settled here. When can I see you?"

"I finish at the bakery at six. I have to run home and shower, but we can go out and celebrate tonight."

"What are we celebrating?"

"You being here, duh!"

"Great. Can't wait."

"Tanner and I will pick you up later. I'm so happy you're here. I can't wait to see you. It will be just like old times."

Old times. If only. "Text me when you're on your way."

Charlotte has no idea what had happened between me and Joe. She knows we broke up, but I hadn't told her the rest. I wasn't ready to talk about it then. Honestly, I'm still not.

I'm not sure when I will be.

———

CHARLOTTE'S FRIEND, MALLORY, HAS NOT STOPPED TALKING SINCE the second I got into the car.

I force a laugh here and there, nodding like I'm listening. But all I can focus on is the text that just came through on my phone.

. . .

JOE: I HOPE YOU MADE IT TO NY SAFELY. CAN WE PLEASE TALK when you get home? I miss you.

A HUNDRED DIFFERENT RESPONSES BOUNCE AROUND MY BRAIN. I don't type any of them because I don't want him to see those dreadful dots show up on his screen. What is there to talk about? Unless Joe has the DeLorean, there's no way he can fix this sans time travel.

By the time we're inside the bar doing shots, I've reread Joe's message five times. (And Mallory's still talking.)

My mom was right: Joe is young. Young people make mistakes. But when a mistake breaks a heart in the process, how do you find forgiveness amidst the wreckage? Joe left me when things got real. Not only did he run, but he ran into the arms of another woman. How could he say he loves me, yet hurt me so badly?

"And this is my best friend, Carla."

The sound of my name snaps my attention up from my phone to see who Charlotte is introducing me to. We're meeting one of Tanner's friends tonight, though I don't remember his name since I was only half-listening.

Tattoos. Muscles. Piercing blue eyes. Lips curved into a cocky smile. Holy Mother of Dragons, *it's him!*

TJ knows Charlotte.

Charlotte knows TJ.

They're *friends.*

My best friend is friends with the man who screwed me so good I have bruises on my hips. So much for my one- night stand with a stranger never to be seen again.

When it comes to fight versus flight, I am a definite flight-risk. But I can't run now. Not without seeming like a certified lunatic. Like any sane person, I resort to telepathy. I'm not sure how it works, but I'm hoping to convey a message that says *don't you dare breathe a word to anyone about last night.*

It must've worked because TJ extends his hand and says, "Nice to meet you, Carla." If only he wasn't wearing that shit-eating grin.

My teeth grind together as I plaster on a smile and slip my hand into his. The molecules in the air around us crackle. "Nice to meet you." My eyes zoom in on his tattooed fingers as they wrap around my hand. I recall the way they looked when they were sliding between my —*no*. Focus.

I'm so distracted by the explosions going off in my head, I miss half the conversation that follows our introduction.

Mallory grips my arm. "You should move here. I'd totally get an apartment with you. I'm dying to get out of my house."

Charlotte looks offended. "Why didn't you ask me to get an apartment with you?"

Mallory points her thumb at Tanner. "You're moving in with him."

"I never said that!"

Mallory rolls her eyes. "You will eventually, and I can't carry the rent on my own when you do."

My mouth is finally able to form words. "You're looking to move out?" I don't know if I could tolerate living with someone as loud as Mallory, so I add that to the con side of my mental list. But on the pro side, having someone to split the rent with would definitely make things easier. Wait, why am I thinking about moving here? Do I want to move here?

Mallory's face lights up. "Hell, yes! Let me know and I'll start apartment hunting."

Tanner hugs Charlotte to his side. "See, babe? Your friends are going to live together. We should live together. Everybody wins."

"And when you guys start fighting, I can tell you to come stay at my place." Mallory turns to me. "They've broken up at least five times since they started dating."

Charlotte's hand flies to her hip. "That's an exaggeration."

"Bullshit," TJ fake coughs.

"You're together now," I say. "That's all that matters." I lift my index finger to Tanner's nose and step closer to him. "But if you break her heart, I'll kill you."

Tanner raises his right hand. "I will never hurt her."

That's what they all say.

"Feisty and beautiful," TJ says. "I like your friend, Charlotte."

Sex with TJ flashes through my mind again. From the three different times we'd had sex. In three different positions. My favorite being when he was behind me and—*no*. Get it together.

I pull Charlotte and Mallory toward the dance floor. "Let's dance." I push my way through the crowd and find a spot for us to squeeze into.

"You know TJ was just being nice," Charlotte shouts over the music.

"I'm just not in the mood."

Mallory's eyebrows shoot up. "Not in the mood for *that?*"

"I just want to forget about men for tonight and enjoy my time with you girls." And stop thinking about TJ's tattooed hands all over my skin.

Charlotte splits her time dancing between us and Tanner. He seems like a good guy and she looks truly happy with him. All because she took a chance in a new town.

If she was able to start a new life here, maybe I could do the same.

Mallory turns out to be pretty fun. We tear up the dance floor, rolling our hips and shaking our asses to every song. It would be nice to live with someone who's also single. That gets added to the pro column.

TJ doesn't leave his spot at the bar as he tortures himself with another glass of whiskey. I know this because my attention keeps pulling in his direction. Part of me feels bad for ignoring him and wants to go sit with him. But that would draw too much attention and I don't want to answer the questions Charlotte will have.

Mallory returns from the bar with another round of shots. "So Charlotte told me your boyfriend broke up with you."

"He did."

"You'll find someone else. Forget about him."

I clink my glass against hers. "Cheers to that." The sweet liquid rolls down my throat. Forgetting about him is exactly what I plan to do.

One shot of tequila turns into *'Let's do another,'* which turns into *'How many shots have we done?'* We drink until I reach the perfect level of buzzed. Loose enough to not care, stable enough to walk.

Mallory points across the room. "See that chick over there with the curly hair?"

"Pretty girl. Who is she?"

"That's the girl TJ's in love with."

"Who's that tall blond dude she's cozied up with?"

"That's her boyfriend, Chase." Mallory shakes her head. "TJ was training her at his gym. He fell in love. She didn't."

I steal another glance in TJ's direction. He's talking with the bartender, who's giggling and doing that thing girls do when they push their boobs together with their elbows. "He can get any girl he wants. I'm sure he'll be fine."

"That man is sex on a stick. A very big stick."

"More like a tree."

"A tree I'd like to climb ... naked."

Naked. Naked with TJ. A shiver runs down my spine and my thighs involuntarily squeeze together. Is sex with a stranger always that good? Something tells me it's not. I think I just got lucky. The way he touched me, every kiss, every caress ... it didn't feel raunchy, the way I'd always thought casual sex would be. It felt empowering. Sensual. As if TJ and I connected on a deeper level.

"Are you okay?" Mallory asks. "You're dripping sweat."

Oh, I'm dripping more than just sweat. I need to cool off, can't breathe. "I'm going to get some air. I'll be back."

I push through the sea of sweaty people and out the door. The air outside isn't much better, thick with humidity, but the slight breeze cools my damp skin. I gather my hair and twist it around itself to air out my neck.

I lean against the building as I watch couples walk to their cars, holding hands and shouting goodbyes to friends across the parking lot. They all look happy. Carefree. I used to look like that. Will I ever feel that way again? Will there come a day when I don't wake up thinking about the baby I lost? The love I lost? The life I almost had?

"It's not much cooler out here."

I jump at the sound of TJ's voice.

"Sorry. Didn't mean to scare you. What are you doing out here?"

I release my hair and fluff it with my fingers. "Just wondering if everyone is happy with their lives."

"They're all drunk."

"Not just them. You know what I mean."

"Doesn't really matter what other people are. Are *you* happy, Carla?"

I feel like I don't know how to be anymore. Heartbreak is like losing a limb. You have to relearn how to do all the things you used to do when you had your appendage. Now, everything's harder. Everything serves as a reminder of what you lost.

"You need to move on," TJ says when I don't answer. "Life doesn't always go as planned."

"Then what's the point?"

"That *is* the point. You can't plan for everything. Gotta roll with the punches as they come."

"Great. Another fighting metaphor." I shake my head and bite my tongue to keep from saying everything else that wants to come out. He might be in love with someone who doesn't love him back, but he doesn't know the kind of pain I've experienced. He couldn't possibly understand.

"Please don't tell Charlotte anything. Not what I told you about getting pregnant, and definitely not about last night."

"I won't," he says, and for some reason I believe him. "But why don't you want to talk to her? She's your best friend."

"I will. I just haven't found the right time. I didn't want to bother her when she first came back. She went through so much."

"So did you."

I shrug. "I'll be fine."

"Yeah, you will." He stands in front of me, ducking his head until I look at him. "You're lucky your ex showed you his true colors before you married him. Not much of a man if he abandons his wife-to-be when shit gets real. I say he did you a favor."

I tilt my head, letting that thought settle in my brain. "That's a good way of looking at it."

"See? It's not so bad opening up to a handsome stranger."

I roll my eyes, but I'm smiling. That's the effect TJ has on a person. So charming it's irritating. So adorable you don't know if you want to smack him or kiss him. So much wiser than you, you almost can't stand it. *Almost.*

"How long are you here for?" he asks.

"Until Wednesday."

TJ tugs my elbow and guides me around the corner of the building where the streetlight doesn't reach us. We're tucked into the shadows, away from the noise, away from everyone.

"What are you—"

TJ claims my mouth, kissing me hard. My willpower snaps like a rubber band. His lips are addicting, and I crave the familiar taste. I know what it leads to and I know I want more.

"Wanna turn our one-night stand into two?" TJ's mouth trails down my neck, licking, biting, and teasing, reminding me of just how good that mouth can feel.

Do I want to? *God, yes.* Should I? I'm not sure. One more night couldn't hurt, could it?

A throat clears behind us and I jump back.

Tanner's eyes are wide. "Sorry to interrupt, but the girls are ready to leave. Are you coming with us, Carla?"

Both of them look at me expectantly, forcing me to look within myself. *What on earth am I doing? Was I seriously going for round two with TJ?*

"I'm coming with you guys," I say.

Tanner nods and fist-bumps TJ before jogging back to his car.

"I could give you a ride," TJ offers.

"No, thanks. I should go." *Far, far away from you and your muscles.*

"Goodbye, Carla."

"Bye, TJ."

Chapter Eight

THE PAST

T

THE DAY MOM DIED, I THOUGHT MY PROBLEMS WERE OVER. (HOW fucked up does *that* sound?) I had no idea it wasn't the end of my troubles. It was only the beginning.

I'm in the same police station I'd practically grown up in. Except now, I'm not sitting in a detective's chair giving my statement. I'm sitting in a jail cell. And Woods isn't looking at me with those gentle, sorrow-filled eyes. He's looking at me in disgust.

It's ironic, really.

"Woods, hurry up and say whatever you're going to say. I've got a pounding headache and I need to take a piss." At least, that's what I meant to say. What came out was a slurred, mumbled version of that. A bottle of Jack Daniels and a hit of heroin will do that to you.

High is my preferred state now. Being sober after what I'd been through? Impossible. I'd tried.

But I was angry at my father for doing what he did.

Angry at my mother for allowing it to happen.

Angry about having to live with complete strangers who didn't give two shits about me.

Worst of all, I'm angry at myself. Losing control of your own life is a scary thing. You become desperate, willing to try anything and everything to sit in the driver's seat again.

Heroin gave that feeling back to me.

Now, I'm in control. It sounds like an oxymoron, being in control by losing control. But to me, it makes sense. I get high to numb the pain. I'll always be grateful for that redhead.

"Oh, I'm not going to say anything," Woods says. "I'm past saying something."

"Then let me out of here."

"So you can go where, exactly? You've got nowhere else to go. Phil and Theresa aren't going to take you back after this. They were nice people. You could've had a family. A normal life. But you insist on fucking it up every chance you get."

I gesture to the homeless man sleeping on the floor in the corner of the cell. "I think Old Man Jenkins here shit his pants. Just let me out."

"I'm not letting you out of here! Not until you stop this. You can stay in there and rot for all I care."

I roll my eyes. "You can't keep me in here. I'm only seventeen."

He grips the bars and presses his face against them. "I can do whatever the fuck I want!"

I laugh. He looks like he's reenacting that scene from *The Shining* when that guy sticks his face through the door. *Who was that actor?* I can see his face but I can't remember his name.

Woods turns red. "I can't watch this anymore, Thomas. I can't watch you turn into your father."

That stings a little, even in my inebriated state. "I didn't kill anybody. Chill out. And for the hundredth time: stop calling me Thomas."

"You stole money out of Theresa's wallet and pawned her wedding ring. She doesn't want you in her house anymore. This was the last straw."

I whistle with a twirl of my finger in the air. "It should've been the last straw when I fucked her niece, don't you think? Why does a couple hundred dollars from her wallet rank higher on that list?"

"How many more foster homes are you going to get kicked out of before you learn? How many times are you going to shoot up before you die?" He runs a hand through his thinning hair. "Christ, look at all the track marks on your arms. Your mother is rolling over in her grave as we speak."

I flinch at the mention of my mother. That sobers me right the fuck up, which is a problem because I'm not pleasant when I'm sober. I stalk over to where Woods is standing. "My mother isn't doing shit because she's dead. She's fucking dead. You don't know what it's like. You had a perfect life. Your parents loved you, loved each other. You've never had to live in a foster home. I'm better off on the streets than I am with those fucking people."

"Well, that's exactly where you're headed. The fucking streets. You should get used to the smell of your cellmate's shit because that's all you're going to smell when you're living amongst homeless people."

"Jack Nicholson!"

Woods blinks. "What?"

"The actor who was in *The Shining*. It was Jack Nicholson." I chuckle. "Here's Johnny!"

"You're hopeless," Woods murmurs, scrubbing a hand over his face. "Fucking hopeless. I can't help you." He backs away from the bars. "I can't help you anymore."

"I don't need your help. I don't need anyone's help. Just leave me the fuck alone."

I watch Woods walk away until he's out of sight. I lie down on the cold, hard floor and let what's left of my high completely overtake my senses.

I always knew Woods would give up on me. Always knew the end of my line would come.

I just didn't know how much it would hurt.

Chapter Nine

THE PRESENT

arla

"ANYBODY HOME?"

The drumline on the stairs is my only warning. I set my suitcase down and plant my feet firmly on the laminate.

Sam and Lucas, my much-younger brothers, charge at me once they reach the bottom of the staircase. I brace myself for impact.

"Carla's home!" they shout, slamming into me.

I tuck each of them under my arms and spin them around as fast as I can.

"Spin cycle!"

Sam's a squirmer, so I lose hold of him first. He tumbles onto the floor and Lucas goes rolling after him.

"Your heads! Watch your heads!" Mom enters the living room and throws her arms around me. "Oh, honey. I'm so glad you're home. I was so worried about you driving all that way by yourself."

"It was fine, Mom. I actually enjoyed the ride."

Dad breezes past me and sits in his favorite recliner. "Car run okay?"

"It was great until the AC shit the bed."

"Shit the bed! Shit the bed!" the twins chant, now wrestling next to the coffee table.

My hand clamps over my mouth. "Sorry, Mom."

She holds her head and takes a seat on the recliner beside Dad. Her level of melodrama always rises when the boys wrestle.

I sit on the floor cross-legged and make eye-contact with Dad.

"Mr. Andrews is holding your job," he says.

"About that." I clear my throat. "I did a lot of thinking on my drive."

"Good, honey." Mom smiles. "Have you spoken to Joe?"

"No, Mom. I haven't spoken to Joe. I'd appreciate it if you don't speak to him either."

Her lips form a straight line.

"What were you thinking about?" Dad asks.

My breath is shaky as I inhale. "Well, I've been thinking about moving to New York."

Mom gasps right on cue. "Carla, you can't be serious."

Dad's quiet, watching the twins chase each other around the dining room table.

"I'm serious, Mom. I ... I don't want to stay here anymore. Charlotte made a new life in New York, and she's happy. I'd have her there with me."

"But that's so far from home."

"It's a quick plane ride. We would visit each other."

"Where would you go to school?" Dad asks.

"At the community college Charlotte goes to."

"Where would you live?"

"I'd get an apartment. Charlotte's friend, Mallory, said she'd be my roommate."

"And work?"

"I can work at the bakery with Charlotte."

Dad's quiet again. I prepared myself for his questions. I know how his mind works, because mine works the same way. If he can't find a flaw in the logistics, he can't argue.

"It sounds like you've already made up your mind." Mom's shoulders slump forward, the worry lines deep between her eyebrows.

"You guys have your hands full here with the boys. I had a plan but it got all messed up. Now it's time for me to figure out a new one."

"And you need to be all the way in New York to do that?"

I shrug. "There's only one way to find out."

"When will you go?"

"I'd have to deregister from the classes I signed up for. Luckily they haven't started yet, so I won't lose any money. Mallory's apartment hunting so I guess it depends how long it takes her to find one."

Dad nods. "You should use some of the money Nana left you to help with the deposit."

A disgusted sound leaves Mom's throat as she stands. "You're discussing this like it's just some business transaction."

"She's moving. It *is* a business transaction."

"Our baby girl is leaving us, Robert."

"I heard her, Beth. But she's not a baby anymore. She's grown. She won't stay with us forever."

Mom pouts and sits back down. Dad rubs her back in small circles. Though he isn't one for affection, he knows what Mom needs.

They're completely opposite from one another, yet they work so well together. *Will I ever have what they have?* I always thought I'd have lasting love with Joe. Now, who knows what my future holds? I'm about to embark on a new adventure. I'm not sure what's in store for me, and it's terrifying.

The beautiful, dark stranger pops into my mind, and a smile creeps onto my face.

Plan A didn't work out, so now you move on to Plan B.

———

Deregister from my classes. *Check.* Contact the College of Staten Island about enrollment. *Check.* Find an apartment. *Check.* Call Joe back ... *question mark.*

I haven't been able to cross that one off yet, and it's killing me. I hate not being able to complete a to-do list.

I've been staring at Joe's name on my phone for the past three weeks. Since I'd returned from New York, he'd left thirty-two texts and three voicemails. Mom says I should talk to him. Part of me wants to get it over with. But every time I think I'm going to make the call, something interrupts me.

Take yesterday, for example. I was about to call him when I realized my bookshelf needed to be reorganized. I'd had my books in alphabetical order by title, but the genres were all different. Clearly, they couldn't remain in disarray like that. It feels so much better now that I have Colleen Hoover sitting between Jamie McGuire and Kandi Steiner.

The day before that, I sat down with every intention to call Joe, but *Bridesmaids* was on the E! channel. When that movie comes on, one doesn't turn it off. One sits there and recites every line from the airplane scene.

"Stove. What kind of name is that? Are you an appliance?" It gets me every time.

Two days prior, I cleaned out Mom's pantry and grouped her spices in order of how often she uses them. I'm not paying rent here, so I need to help out whenever I can.

What I'm trying to say is: I've been extremely busy doing very important things.

Now, I sit on my bed with my phone in hand. No interruptions. No distractions. It's time. I take a deep breath as my thumb hovers over Joe's name.

I'm feeling anxious. Maybe I should do yoga before I call Joe. Then, I'll be more relaxed when we talk. I set my phone on my night stand and roll out my mat.

Thirty minutes later, I'm on my back in Corpse Pose. My eyes survey my childhood bedroom. The Backstreet Boys poster still taped to the wall. The first-place soccer trophy on top of the bookcase. The collage of selfies Charlotte and I had taken over the years. The Georges Seurat painting hanging above my bed. If someone who didn't know me stepped into my room, he or she would be able to learn about who I am. The things I like, at the very least.

I can't help but think how much different it looks from TJ's bare bedroom. No pictures. No artwork. Just the essentials. Maybe that's how men like it, but my gut tells me there's more to it than that.

My mind drifts to thoughts of TJ whenever I think about my move. I also think of him before I fall asleep at night, but that's for a *much* different reason.

He's so strong, so self-assured. The man had an answer for everything I'd told him, as if my problems aren't problems at all. As if everything's trivial.

Maybe everything is.

Maybe I've had it wrong all this time.

Plan A didn't work out, so now you move on to Plan B.

An idea sparks. I roll up my yoga mat, sit at my desk, and flip to a clean page in my notebook. I scribble a new list:

Plan B
- Move to New York
- Graduate college
- Get a job
- Go sky diving
- Get a tattoo
- Volunteer

I ADD ONE MORE ITEM TO MY LIST, JUST BECAUSE I'VE ALREADY DONE it and I can cross it off:

- ~~Have a one- night stand~~

IF I'M STARTING OVER, I NEED TO CHANGE MORE THAN JUST MY location. I need to change my outlook. My habits. My ways.

It's time to rebuild myself from the ground up.
Now I just have to figure out how.

Chapter Ten

THE PAST

"GONNA BE A BRUTAL ONE TONIGHT."

I rub my hands together over the fire. "Gotta love winters in New York."

"One of my buddies didn't make it last winter. We had that bad blizzard. He never met us back at the shelter. Died in the street and the snow just covered him. The plow wound up pushing his body all the way down to Times Square before someone found him."

"Shit."

Steve keeps talking, telling stories like he always does. He's been homeless for ten years. Not exactly something to brag about, but when you've got nothing, you cling to anything to feel like you've got something.

In the year since Woods and I last spoke, I've been kicked out of three more foster homes. Expelled from two more schools. In and out of juvie. But once I turned eighteen ... that was it. The revolving door stopped. There was only one place left for me to go.

Life's been tough, but none of it compares to being homeless. This is rock bottom.

I'd go back to getting beat on by fatass Dave if I could. Crazy, isn't it?

Homeless.

Not a word I thought I'd ever be associated with. Yet here I am, standing over a rusty old garbage can trying to keep warm. I'm even wearing a pair of fingerless gloves to complete my look.

"Hey, TJ. Let me introduce you to my friend. This is Bobby. He runs the underground fights here in the city."

Bobby shoves him and Steve falls on his ass. "What the fuck, Steve? You can't go runnin' your mouth, tellin' people about fighting."

I stifle a laugh.

"Somethin' funny to you, string bean?" Bobby walks over to where I'm standing and folds his arms over his chest. The dude is pretty muscular for someone who's homeless. Wonder where he's getting fed.

I shake my head. "Steve just broke the first rule of Fight Club."

A slow smile stretches across Bobby's face. "Kid's got jokes. What's your name, son?"

"Well, it's not string bean. And I'm not your son. You can call me TJ."

"I'll call you whatever the fuck I want to call you. Look at you, mouthin' off to me like you know somethin'." His arms spread wide. "Why don't you show me what you know?"

"No, thanks," I say, turning away from the fire. "I'm not interested in your little fight club."

"You not interested in makin' money?"

I stop and turn around. "Money?"

"What do you think we're fightin' for, string bean? Winner gets paid fifty perfect. I get the other fifty. Loser goes home empty-handed. Or in a body bag."

"How much are you talking?"

"Don't matter if you're not interested in my *little* fight club."

"I'm interested if I'm making money."

"You only make money if you win." Bobby touches his chin while he considers me. "From the looks of you, you ain't winnin'."

"You shouldn't judge a book by its cover. Then again, from the looks of you, you ain't readin'."

Bobby laughs, revealing several missing teeth. "All right, smartass. Come down to the ring tonight. Steve will take you. Show you how to get in. Then we'll see if you make me any money."

———

"HERE ARE THE RULES," BOBBY SHOUTS. "NO WEAPONS OF ANY KIND. If you get knocked out, or tap out, the fight is over. Other than that, anythin' goes."

This guy is seriously on a Brad Pitt power trip. Think he memorized the entire script from *Fight Club*?

It's after midnight. Steve led me downtown to a building that's under construction. Inside, we were escorted down a flight of stairs into the basement.

Roughly one hundred spectators stand around a makeshift octagon —metal barricades to separate the crowd from the fighters. Men in expensive suits with shiny watches shout over each other as everyone places their last-minute bets.

I need that money.

"Tonight, we got a newbie goin' up against Destroyer."

Destroyer? There's no way in hell I'd go by a dumbass name like that.

The crowd boos as I climb over the barricade. I flip them off and they boo louder. I don't need fans. Just need their cash.

My opponent jumps over the barricade and stalks toward me, fists raised in front of his face. He's got about a buck fifty on me and at least six inches in height. I don't know a damn thing about boxing, but I've been in enough fights to know when I'm going to lose.

Tonight, I'm definitely going to lose.

I'm not nervous though. I didn't come here thinking I'd win. You don't need to win a fight to prove yourself. All you need is heart. Tenacity. I'm underestimated because of my size, but what they don't know is that I've got nothing to lose.

And that's the most dangerous kind of person.

I last all three rounds with Destroyer. I got a few good shots in, but he pretty much rearranged my face. Totally get his nickname now. I think my jaw is broken.

But when he's declared the winner, I'm still standing and ready for more. Random people in the crowd clap me on the back, and Bobby asks me to fight for him again.

"We need to beef you up, string bean."

"Then I need to get fed," I say.

"I'll see what I can do about that."

Chapter Eleven

THE PRESENT

arla

"Pivot! Pivot!"

"Stop making me laugh. I can't breathe." I set my end of the table down and double over.

Mallory drops her end and wipes her eye with the back of her hand. "That is one of my favorite *Friends* episodes. It's never not funny."

"Come on. We're almost there." I grunt lifting the table again. "How much did you say you paid for this?"

"I didn't. My neighbor bought a new table for his dining room so he put this one out on the curb."

"I can't believe someone would throw this out. It's in great condition. Once we decide on a color scheme, I can paint it to match."

"Who knew I'm living with Picasso over here? This is gonna be awesome."

"Painting furniture hardly makes me Picasso."

We reach the top of the stairs and carry the table into the dining room. Our dining room. In our new apartment.

Mallory's right. This is going to be awesome.

"Hello? Anybody home?" Charlotte's head pops through the doorway.

"In here!"

"This place looks great." Charlotte wraps me in a hug. "I'm so happy you're living here. We're going to have so much fun."

Tanner walks inside carrying two of the chairs from our dining set. "How did you guys get that table up the stairs? I wish you would've called me."

"Pfft." Mallory waves her hand. "We are strong, independent women who don't need no man! Besides, Carla's a beast."

I flex my bicep and wink.

"Well, I'm impressed." TJ's voice rips through me like a shockwave.

I whirl around and lock eyes with him. "What are *you* doing here?"

He grins. "Nice to see you too. We came to help, but it looks like you ladies have it handled."

"The sofa's still down in the truck. You guys can make yourselves useful." Mallory snaps her fingers. "We'll organize the kitchen."

TJ and Tanner salute her and trot down the stairs.

"What's up with you two?" Charlotte asks.

I hike a shoulder, tearing into a box labeled *Kitchen*. "Nothing."

"You're so weird around him."

"I'm not weird. You're weird."

"Good one, comeback queen." Mallory nudges me with her elbow. "Are you a lesbian?"

Charlotte smacks her forehead. "Mal! We already went over this. You can't go around asking people if they're gay."

"Why not?"

"Because ... you just can't."

"I think I need to know if my roommate plans on ogling my goodies while I'm in the shower."

I laugh. "I'm not a lesbian. Your goodies are safe. TJ just ... isn't my type."

"Hot as hell with abs carved out of stone isn't your type?"

Charlotte stifles a giggle. "Carla likes the clean-cut guys."

"Ah, so you like them safe." Mallory scrunches her nose. "Safe is boring. Know what my motto is?"

"I really need to get laid?"

Mallory flings an oven mitt at me. "No. My motto is: Better sorry than safe. You won't have any fun in life if you're always playing it safe."

"I second that," Charlotte adds.

I once thought Joe was safe. Look how that turned out. Maybe Mal's on to something.

The boys are back with the couch, putting an end to the conversation. My traitorous eyes watch the muscles work under TJ's skin as he passes us on the way to the living room. The T-shirt with cut-off sleeves he's wearing gives me a clear shot at his lean, shredded obliques. The tattoos flow from one to the next, telling a story I can't quite make out. His body is like a painting you want to stare at for hours, studying each and every brush stroke in awe.

It's been a month since our sexcapades, yet my skin still ignites in his presence.

Mallory hands me a paper towel.

"What's this for?"

"To wipe your drool."

I shove her with a smirk.

"Where do you want this?" TJ calls.

"Oh, I'll show him where I want it." Mallory wiggles her eyebrows before heading into the living room.

Charlotte shakes her head. "She is insufferable."

"She's like a horny frat boy."

"She's a good friend though. I can't believe my two best friends are living together. How do you feel?"

"A little nervous being in a new city, but I'm excited."

"I can show you around this weekend. I'll help you look for jobs too."

"I was hoping I could work at the bakery with you and Mal. I'll scrub toilets, work weekends. Whatever you need."

Charlotte chews her bottom lip. "We already hired two people this summer. I don't know if Dad can afford to take you on right now."

Disappointment settles in the pit of my stomach. "Oh, that's okay. I'll find something else."

"I can talk to Dad and see what he says."

"No." I wave my hand. "It's totally fine. Don't worry about me."

"You looking for a job?" TJ says as he emerges from the living room with Tanner and Mallory.

"Something that can work around my class schedule."

"I have a few positions I'm looking to fill at my gym."

"I'm sure Carla would love any position you put her in." Mallory winks before ripping open another box.

If looks could kill, there would be a dead body on the floor of our new kitchen. Too bad she won't make eye contact with me to see it before she dies.

TJ just smirks. *Cocky bastard.* "Why don't you come by at seven tonight? I can show you around and we can talk."

Pro: I'd have a job.

Con: The man I had mind-blowing sex with would be my boss.

Pro: Maybe we'll have mind-blowing sex again.

Con: No, no, no. That is a very bad idea.

"Fine," I say. "I'll be there at seven."

———

AT 6:55PM, I'M STANDING INSIDE TJ'S GYM. NO ONE IS BEHIND THE front desk so I walk around, taking it all in. Thick ropes, weight racks, giant tires, and punching bags line the perimeter of the large warehouse. The gym seems empty.

Then I spot him. The octagon-shaped ring is toward the back of the room. The overhead lights act as spotlights on the two contenders circling each other. TJ's opponent only reaches his waist. The boy can't be more than seven-years old. He's wearing headgear, fingerless boxing gloves, and a mouth guard that's stretching his small lips to their limit. The sleeves of his shirt are cut off to match TJ's.

"Jab, jab, swing!" TJ yells.

The boy fires a series of punches at the large red pad TJ holds.

"Nice. Again!"

Jab, jab, swing.

TJ drops the pad and ruffles the boy's thick hair. "Great work today, Michael. Have a seat."

Michael tosses his headgear and mouthpiece onto the floor. The two sit, and the boy crisscrosses his legs like TJ.

"What happened at school today?"

Michael shrugs and averts his eyes to his toes.

"Your dad said you got sent to the principal's office. Is that true?"

Michael nods.

"What happened, Michael? I need you to talk to me."

"Christopher stole my lunchbox and dumped my food onto the floor. Everyone saw."

"Then what happened?"

"I punched him like you taught me to."

TJ touches his finger to Michael's chin, lifting his face to make eye contact. "I don't teach you to hurt people. You know that."

"But Christopher is a bully! Someone has to teach him a lesson. I'm tired of getting picked on."

"It's not your job to teach him a lesson. It's your job to worry about yourself. Keep yourself out of trouble. Punching a bully doesn't fix the problem."

"I'm just a kid. How am I supposed to fix the problem?"

"You're not just a kid. You're powerful. You're smart. You can do more than you think. But you can't go around punching everyone who's mean to you. Otherwise, Dad won't let you train with me anymore. Do you understand that what you did was wrong?"

"Yes," Michael says, groaning. "I should've used my words like you told me to."

"Words are more powerful than you realize. Even more so than your fists. He's picking on you because he's weak. Maybe he's hurting. Maybe his life isn't so great. Maybe he just needs a friend. I say you walk right up to Christopher tomorrow and invite him here."

Michael's eyes go wide. "You want him to come here so you can train him?"

"No. I want him to come here so *you* can train him. I want him to see how awesome you are. But he doesn't have to know that."

A smile spreads across Michael's face. "I like that idea."

"Good. That's your homework. Let's go see if Dad's here."

Michael's shoulders slump. "Can't we practice a few more moves?"

"Sorry, my man. Time's up." TJ stands and holds the bottom rope down with his foot so Michael can climb out of the ring.

Michael's eyes land on me. "Who's she?"

"This is Carla. She might be working here with us."

I smile and wave. "Those were some serious punches you were throwing in there."

Michael's toothy grin lights up his face. "Thanks." He cranes his neck to look at TJ. "You should hire her. She's really pretty."

My mouth drops open and TJ laughs. "She's too old for you, bud."

"But she's not too old for you."

"What are you, a matchmaker?" He nudges Michael's rear end with his foot. "Go see if your dad is outside."

Michael takes off toward the door.

"You're early." TJ wipes the sweat from his forehead with a towel.

"Aren't you supposed to be punctual for a job interview?"

He grins and spreads his arms out wide. "Welcome to Heavy Weight."

"Why would anyone bully that sweet boy?"

"Kids are cruel. Haven't you ever been picked on?"

I nod as I recall junior high. "You're looking at Clumsy Carla."

"What earned you that nickname?"

"Dad's here," Michael shouts before bolting out the door.

"Shit. Be right back." TJ sprints after him.

I watch through the glass as he kneels down to talk to Michael. Michael throws his arms around TJ's neck, and then climbs into the back seat of his father's car.

"Sorry about that," TJ says, locking the front door and flipping the sign to 'Closed.' "I keep telling him not to run into the street."

"It's okay."

"Let's go to my office."

I follow TJ behind the front desk to a door tucked into the corner. The nameplate on the door reads 'Reggie Hart.'

"Who's Reggie?"

"The previous owner." TJ gestures to the chair in front of his desk and plops into the rolling chair behind it. "So, tell me why the kids called you Clumsy Carla."

"The name's pretty self-explanatory."

"If I'm going to hire you, I need to know how clumsy we're talking. I don't need you injuring yourself and going out on workers' comp." TJ rocks back in his chair, the hint of a smile dancing on his lips.

"Can we just talk about the positions you have available?"

"What, no eye roll?"

"Are you trying to aggravate me?"

"It's easy to do. You're wound so tightly."

"I am not."

"I'm surprised you didn't wear your secretary outfit."

"Are you disappointed?"

TJ's eyes rove over my knee-length black dress. "Hardly."

Heat spreads from my cheeks down my neck and chest.

He clears his throat and returns his eyes to mine. "So, I need someone to man the front desk from three 'til close, Monday through Friday. Roger's been there full-time, but his wife is on bedrest for the next six months and he needs to get his daughter from school."

"I have all morning classes, so my afternoons are free."

"I'm also interested in adding more classes to the schedule here. Something aimed at a different crowd, like a weekly yoga class. See how it goes."

"I do yoga, but I've never been an instructor before. I'm sure you could find someone more qualified than me."

He shrugs. "There will always be someone more qualified than you if you look hard enough. Sleep on it. Let me know your thoughts tomorrow."

"Tomorrow?"

"You start working the front desk tomorrow."

"But you haven't asked to see my resume." I flip open the folder I've been holding and slide it across his desk.

TJ glances at it and laughs. "You actually typed this up for me?"

"You seem to be confused about how an interview is conducted."

His arms fold over his chest. "Enlighten me."

"I show up early. You note my punctuality and my professional appearance. I show you my resume. You look it over to see if I'm qualified for the position based on my experience."

"I don't need a piece of paper to tell me you're qualified."

"You don't?"

"You're high strung, so you'll take the job seriously. I bet you're organized as hell too. You've got a quick mouth, so you won't take shit from anybody in here. And you're gorgeous."

"What does that have to do with anything?"

"Guys always want to go to a gym that has a pretty face working behind the desk."

I scoff. "That's offensive."

"I didn't say your looks got you the job. I called you organized and smart. Didn't you hear anything I just said?"

"You said my looks would bring in customers. This isn't Hooters."

TJ scrubs a hand over his face. "Fine. I take it back. You're ugly as sin and you'll scare everyone away from my business. That better?"

"Much."

He chuckles and opens a drawer in his desk. Pulling out a shirt, he tosses it at me. "This is what you'll wear. Pants can be jeans, sweats, yoga pants. Whatever you prefer. I don't care as long as your ass isn't hanging out of your shorts. I like to keep things professional here."

I raise an eyebrow, feeling the need to address the elephant in the room. "Then it should go without saying that we can't do the things we did last month. Ever again."

"We fucked, Carla. You can say it."

"Whatever you want to call it, we can't let that happen if I'm going to work for you. That was a one-time thing. And very uncharacteristic of me."

"Don't you want to ask me about how much I'm going to pay you?"

"For the sex?"

"For the job. Get your head out of the gutter, love."

My cheeks flame. "Oh. Right. That's what I thought you meant."

"It'll be fifteen an hour. That's $300 a week. If you teach a class, you'll get more, of course."

Pro: It's more than minimum wage and I'd start tomorrow.

Con: My boss knows what I look like naked.

But I just moved into an apartment and need an income. Against my better judgement, I nod and stand.

"I'll see you tomorrow at three."

Chapter Twelve

THE PAST

J

"Gentlemen, I give you the winner of tonight's fight: TJ Cutler!"

I raise my arms overhead and the crowd roars.

I bend down to offer my opponent a hand, but he swats me away. "I don't need your fucking help."

"Aww, a sore loser? I haven't met one of those in a while."

He spits blood at my feet. "Fuck you. You don't fight fair."

"Fair?" A laugh rips from my chest. "Nothing's fair in life. The sooner you learn that, the better off you'll be."

Bobby's arm wraps around my shoulders. "Leave this piece of shit here. Take your money and celebrate."

"What am I celebrating?" I take the wad of cash and stuff it into my pocket.

"Another win. That makes twenty in a row." He pushes through the crowd as everyone empties out of the building. "Seems like just yesterday you were a string bean. Look at you now. Meetin' me is the best thing that's ever happened to your sorry ass."

"I'd say you're the lucky one with all the money I've made you this year."

Bobby laughs and slaps me on the back. "Come on. I've got a birthday gift for you."

I follow him around a desk by the front door. "What is this place anyway?"

"Supposed to be a gym. We'll be movin' on to another location for the next fight. Staten Island's got tons of empty buildings." He opens the door in the corner of the room.

I point to the name plate on the door. "Who's Reggie?"

"Who gives a fuck?" He shoves me through the threshold.

In the room are two identical blonds perched on a leather couch. Scantily clad is a severe understatement, their fake tits straining against the thin straps of their tops. My dick twitches at the thought of a threesome, but I spot something else I want even more.

Beside them on the couch is a needle.

"Happy Birthday." Bobby winks before closing the door.

I smile and pick up the needle before sitting between the twins. "Hi, ladies."

"Hi, TJ," they say in unison. One of them ties an elastic band around my arm and takes the needle from me. Let's call her Jessica.

Jessica's sister kneels on the floor and positions herself between my legs, tugging on my shorts. She'll be Delilah for tonight. I lift my hips and she slides my boxers down around my ankles.

Just as the needle pierces my vein, Delilah takes me into her mouth. My head falls back against the couch as the waves of ecstasy roll over me.

Money in my pocket. Food in my stomach. Heroin in my veins. And a tongue around my cock.

I'd say this is the best birthday I've ever had.

————

A KNOCK AT THE DOOR STIRS ME AWAKE. JESSICA AND DELILAH ARE asleep on either side of me. They're naked, clothes strewn about the room, and my pants are still around my ankles. Blurred visions of them on me, me on them, and them on each other whirl through my mind.

The knock turns to pounding. I slip out from under the twins and make myself decent. "I'm coming! Hold your fucking horses." Shoving the remnants of drugs into my pocket, I unlock the door and rip it open.

A man with dark, chocolate skin towers over me. His T-shirt and sweatpants are pulling at the seams trying to contain his muscular physique. The dude is built like Dwayne Johnson. His salt-and-pepper beard is the only hint at his age.

"Who the fuck are you?" I ask.

"The question is who the fuck are *you*?"

"You're the one pounding on the door like you own the place."

"I do own this place. And you're in my office."

I blink. "Your office?"

He shoulders past me and takes in the room's disheveled appearance. He points to the elastic band and spoon on the couch. "Is that heroin?"

"Are you a cop?"

"Do I look like a fucking cop to you?"

"Not the doughnut-eating kind."

The man snorts. "Get this shit cleaned up. I've got work to do." He walks over to his desk in the corner of the room and sits in the rolling chair.

I nudge the twins with my foot. "Time to go, ladies."

The man watches me, shaking his head.

"You got something to say, old man?"

"Old man?" He barks out a laugh. "You think you're a hot shot 'cause you won a few fights in some reject boxing matches? You don't know shit about fighting."

My fists clench at my sides. "You don't know me."

He rises from his chair and stalks around his desk. "You're a junkie who fights for money 'cause he's got nowhere else to go. You're at rock bottom and you think you're going somewhere with this fighting bullshit, but you're not. You're a nothing and you'll always be a nothing."

Okay. Maybe he does know me. "Fuck you. It's easy to judge others when you're sitting pretty in your office. You've probably never had to struggle a day in your life."

The man walks me backward until I'm against the wall. "You think you're the only one who's had a shitty life? The only one whose mama didn't love him or his daddy left? Get your head out of your ass, kid."

I place my hands on his blocky shoulders and push, but the man doesn't budge. I falter backward and my head hits the wall.

"Now you listen here. If you want to go anywhere in life and make something of yourself, the first thing you need to do is get rid of that shit in your pocket." His voice lowers. "Nobody ever succeeds doing that."

"You've got it all wrong. I love my life. I don't need anybody telling me what to do."

"Is that so?" He smirks. "Why didn't you take these two back to your place? Would've been a lot more comfortable in your own bed."

I avert my eyes to the twins still asleep on the couch.

"Exactly." He walks away and relaxes back in his chair. He turns on his computer, slipping a small pair of glasses onto the bridge of his nose.

"Fuck you," I mutter, turning for the door.

"The only person you're fucking here is yourself, kid."

I spin around. "Life fucked me. I didn't ask for any of this. I didn't do anything to deserve this. I'm doing the best I can to make the most out of what I've got."

"If this is your best, I'd hate to see you at your worst."

My arms spread wide. "What the fuck do you suggest I do, oh wise one? Tell me. I'd love to hear your perfect solution."

"Step one is admitting you have a problem."

I laugh. "You're going to put me on some NA steps? That's your solution? Thanks, but no thanks." I turn to leave again.

"I could just call the cops, if you'd prefer."

My body stills in the doorway.

"The drugs and trespassing charges should be enough, but they'll really throw the book at you for participating in illegal gambling at an underground fighting ring."

How does he know about the fighting?

"Then again, maybe you want to go to jail. At least you'd have a bed and three meals a day." He gestures to the twins. "But they don't have *that* in jail."

"Fine. You want me to admit I have a problem? I love heroin. There. I said it."

He shakes his head. "That's not admitting to your problem."

I run my fingers through my hair and let out a puff of air. "I'm addicted to heroin. Are we done now? Can I leave?"

Rocking back in his chair, he folds his arms over his chest and smiles. "You can't leave yet. We're just getting started."

Chapter Thirteen

THE PRESENT

arla

"Why do people always wear overalls when they're painting?"

I look down at my ripped denim overalls and chuckle. "I don't know. It's what they wear in the movies."

"We look too cute to work," Mallory says. "Let's do brunch instead."

I dip the roller into the paint tray. "We can do brunch once our apartment is painted and decorated. We only have a few things left on our list."

"You get way too excited about to-do lists."

"You'll thank me when we have a rockin' apartment."

"Oh, then we can have an apartment-warming party."

"We have a tight two-bedroom apartment. How many people are we talking?"

She waves a hand. "Not a lot."

I raise an eyebrow.

"You'll thank me when our bar is fully stocked from all the alcohol people bring us."

"Fine. Now grab a paint brush and turn the volume up."

For the next few hours, Mallory and I paint each room while gyrating our hips to the top club songs from the 90's. Madonna, La Bouche, and Amber. I mixed in a little Blackstreet for good measure. Mallory loves my playlists and I love making them. We're a match made in roommate heaven.

When 2:30 hits, I'm changing into my work clothes and fixing my hair. I swipe my lashes with mascara and dab on some lip gloss.

"I can't believe you're working for that hunk of a man." Mallory sprawls out on my bed. "I bet you're going to see him with his shirt off."

"He's my boss, Mal. I can't be looking at him without his shirt on."

"Work romances are hot. Does he have a desk?"

"Yes, and we will not be having sex on it."

She grins. "Funny how you knew exactly where I was going with that one."

"Goodbye, Mal."

———

I WALK INTO THE GYM TEN MINUTES EARLY. IT'S MORE CROWDED than it was last night. Several trainers are working with clients around the room and TJ's in the ring with a middle-aged woman.

"You must be Carla." The tall man behind the desk extends his hand. "I'm Roger. It's nice to meet you."

I shake his hand and smile. "You as well. Congrats on the baby."

"Thanks. We're hoping for a boy this time. Keep your fingers crossed for me."

"Too much estrogen in your house?"

"That's putting it mildly." He gestures to the touch-screen register. "Let me show you how to work this thing before I leave."

As I watch Roger navigate the computer, I take note of the stacks of papers covering the counter and form a mental to-do list. Filing system. Folders. Labels. My excitement grows when I think about taking a trip to Staples tonight.

"All right. I've got to get my girl off the bus. Take my number. You can call or text if you have any questions."

I hand Roger my phone as TJ passes by, walking his client to the exit. Droplets of sweat run down his skin and I'm mesmerized by the way his muscles flex when he holds the door open. His damp hair sticks up in all directions, much like it did after we—*no*. Don't think about that.

"TJ's a great boss, and an even better friend," Roger says, following my gaze.

"That so?"

"He'll give you the shirt off his back if you need it. He's a miracle worker. Really turns people's lives around." Roger hands my phone back to me. "See you tomorrow." He strides toward the exit and fist-bumps TJ on his way out.

TJ leans his elbows onto the counter. "Happy First Day. How do you feel?"

"Great. Just have a few questions for you."

He waves for me to follow him. "Step into my office."

Once inside, TJ closes the door behind us. I'm lowering myself to sit when he tears his shirt up and over his head and tosses it onto his desk. He rubs a towel over his damp skin, masculinity and sex radiating off him.

I miss the chair by a fraction of an inch because my eyes are glued to the sculpted body in front of me. My ass bounces onto the floor with a thud.

And I'm mortified.

"Shit, you okay?" TJ offers me his hand but I swat it away.

"I'm fine. I ... uh ... have some ideas I want to ... uh ... run by you."

"Only here for five minutes and you've already got ideas. I knew you'd be perfect for the job."

I smooth my hands over my skirt and sit in the chair, making sure to keep my eyes trained on the floor. The desk. The ceiling. Anywhere but on TJ's beautiful body. "Well, the ... uh ... the desk is a mess. I'd like to get some ... uh ... file folders and organize ..."

"Carla." TJ steps lowers his head until I look up at him. "Are you okay?"

"I'm fine ... I just ... can you please put a shirt on?"

A wide grin spreads across his face. Reaching into a gym bag that's sitting on the floor, he pulls out a dry T-shirt and yanks it over his head. He sits on the corner of the desk, still wearing that smug grin. "That better?"

"You're my boss. It's unprofessional to see you without your clothes on."

"It's only unprofessional if you're looking at me like *that*."

My cheeks heat but I lift my chin, determined not to entertain this conversation. "I just wanted your permission to make things more efficient behind the front desk."

"You have my permission to do whatever you need to do."

"Thank you." I nod and stand.

"Carla, I thought I told you to wear any kind of pants you wanted."

I look down at my red pencil skirt and black kitten heels. The color of the skirt matches the gym's logo on the T-shirt. "Is this not okay?"

"It's totally fine. I like how you knotted the front of the shirt too. Just want to make sure you're comfortable here. It's a gym. You don't have to be so ... secretarial."

"Maybe I like being secretarial."

"Okay."

"Okay."

TJ's steel gaze holds me captive. "Is there anything else you need?"

"Nope. I'm good." I spin around and push against the door. I jiggle the knob and push harder, leaning into it with my hip.

"Pull, Carla."

"Right. Pull." I swing the door open and all but run out of the room. *What the hell is wrong with me?*

TJ's busy with clients for the remainder of the day. The phone rings once, and the only "work" I have to do is greet everyone who walks in. Most of my time is spent separating the piles of paper into smaller, homogeneous piles.

At seven o'clock on the dot, TJ's locking the front door.

I wave my arm Vanna White-style. "Look at all my piles."

He leans over the desk and whistles.

I sling my purse over my shoulder and jingle my keys. "Well, I'm off to Staples."

"That's your big Friday night plan? Staples."

I nod excitedly. "I'll have your front desk running like a well-oiled machine in no time."

"You're buying stuff for the gym?"

"Nothing too crazy. Just need to get a home for these stacks of paper."

TJ pulls keys out of his pocket. "Come on. I'll drive."

"Oh, you don't have to come with me. I'm sure you have better things to do."

"Better than a wild night with office supplies? Pfft."

I roll my eyes and walk around the desk. "Let's go before I change my mind."

Outside, I stop in front of TJ's truck and groan. "Why don't we take my car?"

He shakes his head. "I can drive."

"Jury's still out on that one."

"I'm a very safe driver."

"Says the guy who once tried to run me off the road."

He raises three fingers in the air. "I'll be careful with you in the car. Scout's honor."

Somehow, I doubt he was ever a Boy Scout. I step out of my shoes and toss them into the truck. I already fell on my ass in front of him once today—no need to make that twice. I lift my leg but my skirt doesn't stretch enough to allow me to reach the step.

"Want some help, short stuff?"

The amused tone in his voice only irritates me further. "No. I've got this."

I shimmy the hem of my skirt up my thighs, grip onto the handle, and swing myself into the seat. "And she sticks the landing." I pump my fists into the air for effect.

TJ's laughing as he jogs around to the driver's side. Once we're on our way, he turns to me and says, "So, tell me about yourself."

"What do you want to know?"

"What are you going to school for?"

"Accounting."

His eyebrows shoot up. "Really?"

"I like numbers. Numbers never lie."

"Have you always wanted to be an accountant?"

I shake my head and smile. "When I was a kid, I wanted to be an artist. A painter."

"Do you still paint?"

"If you count the apartment walls, then yes."

"Why not major in art?"

"Because I wouldn't be able to do much with it. I need something practical. Something that pays the bills."

"There's more to life than paying bills, Carla."

"They're called starving artists for a reason. I need a steady income. Security."

TJ's quiet until we arrive. I can tell he doesn't agree with me, but he doesn't get what it's like to struggle just to make ends meet.

TJ parks and hops out of his truck. He waits outside my door, holding out his hand. "Let me help you down."

"You saw me get in. I've got this." I swing my legs out the door.

"I just don't want you to—"

Before he can finish his sentence, my heel slips off the metal step and I fall out of the truck.

TJ catches me, wrapping me in his muscular arms. His lips are in my direct line of vision once again, and his warm breath tickles my skin as he chuckles. "I'm starting to understand why you were called Clumsy Carla."

I push out of his arms and straighten my skirt with a huff.

He kneels down to pick up my shoe and takes my ankle in his hand. Goosebumps spread like wildfire under his gentle touch, and I'm sure he notices.

"There ya go, Cinderella." He examines my leg. "Are you hurt? You didn't twist your ankle, did you?"

"Nothing but a bruised ego."

He stands with a grin. "For the record, I tried to help you."

"For the record, your truck is too high."

"Don't blame the truck."

"I don't. I blame the owner." With a smirk, I whip around and strut toward the store. I can hear TJ chuckling behind me.

Inside, I drag TJ up and down each aisle, filling my cart with all the office essentials. Within ten minutes, we're checked out and back in TJ's truck.

"Have you ever tried New York pizza before?" he asks.

"Not yet."

"Let's go fix that."

While he drives, I steal a glance at him form the corner of my eye. "Why do you have so many tattoos?"

"It's addicting. I got one and kept wanting more."

"Do they all mean something?"

"They do."

"Why don't you have any on your stomach?"

"Not every part of me is covered in ink."

Like your perfectly round right butt cheek. I smile at the image that will be forever etched into my memory.

"You seem very intrigued by my tattoos. Do you have any?"

"Not one."

"Didn't think so."

I hate that he's right. "I'd get one if I found the right one."

"Where would you get it?"

"Not sure. Somewhere I could hide it."

"Why get one if you're going to hide it?"

"What if I don't like it in five years? What if it looks ugly when I get wrinkles? It's just so ... permanent."

"Life's about living in the moment. If you worry about the future too much, you won't ever enjoy anything in the present."

His words nestle into my brain as he pulls up to the pizzeria.

I grab a table and TJ places our order. My stomach growls as I inhale the scent of basil and garlic all around me.

TJ slides into the booth with two bottles of water. "So what did your parents think about you moving up here?"

"My dad just wanted to know that I'd lined up school and a job before I left. My mom's the dramatic one. She'd keep me home with her forever if she could."

TJ smiles. "Any siblings?"

"I was an only child up until the twins were born four years ago. My parents hadn't planned on having another baby, let alone two at the same time." I unlock my phone and hold it up so TJ can see a picture of Sam and Lucas climbing me like a jungle gym.

"You must miss them."

"I do, but it feels good to be out on my own."

A waitress arrives and places a large pie in between us. "Here you go, TJ. Can I get anything else for you?"

"No, thanks, Denise. We're good for now."

The waitress saunters away and TJ hands me the first slice. I bite into it, delicious melty cheese and sauce swirling together, and I close my eyes. *Damn, that's good.*

"Tell me that's not the best pizza you've ever tasted."

"Best. Pizza. Ever." I wipe the grease dripping down my chin. "What about your family? What are they like? Is your dad a fighter too?"

TJ shakes his head and swallows a bite of pizza. "Don't have any family."

"Oh. I'm sorry." That explains why there weren't any pictures in his apartment. Now his whole demeanor has changed. *Way to make it awkward, Carla.* I bite into my pizza again while I figure out how to lighten the mood.

"Carla, look at me. It's okay. I'm fine being on my own. I'm used to it."

"You say it like it doesn't hurt."

"Everything hurts if you give it the power to. You can wallow in it, or you can grow from it and move on."

I lean back, shaking my head in disbelief. "You're like one of those desk calendars that has an inspirational quote for every day of the week. People hate those things, you know."

He chokes back a laugh. "You couldn't hate me, Carla Evans. You don't have it in you. You're too good."

"I'm not sure if I should take that as a compliment or an insult."

"Definitely a compliment."

I squirm under his unwavering gaze. He looks at me as if he can see straight into my core, like all my truths are on display no matter how hard I try to hide them.

"And how did you get to be so wise?"

He smirks. "That's another story for another day."

Chapter Fourteen

THE PAST

I CAN'T BELIEVE I'M DOING THIS.

I clear my throat and wipe my palms on my jeans. "Hey. Uh, my name's TJ. I'm an alcoholic. I'm also a heroin addict." I pause while everyone says, "Hi, TJ," in unison. I fight the urge to roll my eyes. This is so lame.

Reggie nods his head, prompting me to continue from the back row of the church we're in.

Why do people hold these meetings in a church? Is it supposed to make us feel like we're being forgiven for our sins? Or maybe it's supposed to make us feel guilty for what we've done. Catholics love laying on the guilt. I never bought into religion. If there is a God, how could he just stand by and watch all of the horrible things that happen to people?

I clear my throat again. "Fuck, I could use a drink right about now." Everyone chuckles. "Jesus was into wine. There's gotta be a bottle around here somewhere." The crowd laughs louder. "People said they saw him walk on water and shit. My opinion? They were all high as a fucking kite." A few of the guys whistle and clap. I don't know what else to say, so I step down and take my seat in the back.

Reggie shoves me through the door once the meeting is over. "You're not there to do stand-up. If you don't take this shit seriously, you'll never be in control."

"I was nervous. I felt like a jackass."

"Sounded like one too."

"Gee, thanks. Some sponsor you must be."

"Did you think this would be easy? Did you think we'd all hug you and tell you how bad we feel about your horrible life? People in there have some real problems—worse than you, if you can get your head out of your ass long enough to see that."

"I don't see how sitting around with a bunch of fellow rejects is going to help us get better. Public speaking makes everyone nervous. The whole premise of the meeting makes people want to drink and use. Sorry for trying to lighten the mood a little."

He pinches the bridge of his nose. "I don't have time for your shit. If you put in the effort, you'll see results. Trust the process."

"Trust?" I grunt. Yeah, not happening. "Thanks but no thanks. I came to the meeting so you wouldn't call the cops on me. Deal's done."

Reggie shakes his head. "Suit yourself."

I storm down the sidewalk. Reggie can't help me. A meeting can't help me. I'm destined to live a fucked-up life. There's nothing anyone can do.

I'm part of the statistic.

Why bother trying to fight it?

Chapter Fifteen

THE PRESENT

arla

It's half-past eight and I'm calling it a night. I'm supposed to help TJ with something on his computer before I leave, but his office door has been closed since he locked the gym doors at seven.

A client is in his office with him. At least, I think she's a client. Her eyes were red and swollen when she walked in. She looked no older than sixteen. TJ didn't turn her away, even though gym hours had ended. He ushered her into his office without hesitation.

That's TJ. He never seems inconvenienced when people ask him for help. He never says no. He just helps.

Over the past few weeks, I've stayed late each night. I converted almost every stack of paper to electronic files, but TJ needed help understanding how to use the computer. I didn't mind doing extra work after hours. TJ lets me study and do homework while I'm there, so I'm grateful. I'm burning the candle at both ends between classes, work, and studying for classes at work, but it's keeping me busy. Busy means I don't have time to think about much else.

Like the texts and calls I keep getting from Joe. It pains me to hear his sad voice in the messages he leaves, and that only makes me mad. Mad at him for ruining us. Mad at myself for still loving someone who hurt me so much.

I wonder if he'll stop calling, or if I'll eventually cave and answer. Not sure which scenario I'd rather.

I sling my purse on my shoulder, keys in hand, when TJ's office door swings open. The girl is no longer crying as she follows him out, a wad of tissues balled in her fist.

"You did good coming to me tonight." TJ wraps his arm around her shoulders. "I'm proud of you."

She shrugs and looks at the floor. "Thanks."

TJ lets her out and turns to me with an apologetic look. "You didn't have to wait this long."

I hold my hand up. "I was in the middle of something. Don't worry about it."

"Why don't you head home? You can help my computer-illiterate ass tomorrow."

"I don't mind staying a few extra minutes."

TJ smiles. A soft one—one I haven't yet seen. It does things to my insides.

In his office, we wait for his computer to power up. "Was every-thing okay with that girl?" I ask. "She looked really upset when she got here."

"Yeah, she'll be okay. She's a recovering addict."

"Oh. Are you her sponsor?"

"No, but the people who come here know my door is always open if they're having a hard time."

I know nothing about alcohol addiction, so I don't ask the ques-tions I have. I point to the computer instead. "Click on the folder that says *Clients*."

I show him how to alphabetize his client list using an Excel spread-sheet. He catches on quickly, so it doesn't take too long. "Now you click *File*. Then click *Save*."

"Where does it go when you save it? How do I find it when I need it?"

I bite my bottom lip. "You saved it to the *Clients* folder. Look at your desktop and you'll see it."

TJ's eyes narrow as he side-eyes me. "Don't laugh."

I hold my hands up on either side of my head. "I'm not laughing."

"You bite your lip whenever you want to laugh but know you shouldn't. It's a thing you do."

Busted. "I'm sorry. I just can't get over the fact that you own a business and have no idea how to make a spreadsheet. It's like you've never used a computer before."

"I didn't grow up with a computer. Never had the need for one."

"Well, now you know how to make a spreadsheet and save it." I stifle a yawn and glance at the time on the computer screen. "Tomorrow, we're getting crazy. I'll show you how to print something."

"I'm sorry for keeping you here so late."

"Stop apologizing. It's fine."

"What are you doing tonight?" he asks.

"Taking a bath. Reading."

"You should go out. It's Friday night. You're young."

"You say it like you're old."

"I am old."

I roll my eyes. "You're not that old. You're twenty-five, not seventy-five."

"And you're nineteen. You should be going to college parties and dancing with boys."

"Is that what you did?"

"Yeah, I danced with all the boys."

I laugh and nudge him with my elbow. "You know what I mean."

"I didn't go to college." He brushes lint off his shorts. "Couldn't afford it."

"Oh." I should just insert my foot in my mouth any time I feel the urge to ask him anything. "Well, I'd rather be here. There's so much organizing I can do."

His eyes flick to my lips for a moment so brief, I wonder if I imagined it. "Is that why you're here? To organize?"

"That ... and I want to help you."

"Why?"

"Roger said something when I started working here. He said you'd give someone the shirt off your back if he needed it."

TJ shrugs it off and averts his eyes to his hands as he folds them in his lap. As confident-bordering-arrogant as he can be, there's another side to him. Modest. Unaware of his greatness. I'm fascinated by this hidden layer.

"I've only known you for a short time, but I get the feeling that people don't do much for you in return." I laugh, trying to keep it light. "Even Superman needs help sometimes."

TJ's eyes close and when they open again, they're blue flames blazing into mine. They hold me captive, and all I can do is try to remember how to breathe. The memory of his lips on mine, his hands all over my body—the memory I work so hard to push from my mind whenever I'm around him—is now all I see.

Heat spreads over my skin like it's following a trail of gasoline leading straight between my thighs. I shift in my seat, trying to suppress the ache. The itch I shouldn't scratch.

When TJ's gaze falls to my lips again, my breath hitches. He's going to kiss me.

And I'm going to let him.

He leans in and stops a centimeter from my face. I'm ready to close the gap when he says, "You should probably go."

"Oh, right." I stand so fast my chair wobbles behind me.

"Carla, wait."

"I'm sorry. Good night." I'm out the door and in my car in the matter of seconds.

I don't allow myself to dissect what just happened—what I wanted to happen. TJ is my boss and I can't almost-kiss my boss. It won't happen again. And that's the end of that. My ego can't take anything more.

When I arrive at my apartment, I drag my legs up the stairs. As soon as I turn the key in the door, the smell hits me.

Something's burning.

I rush into the kitchen to find Mallory waving a towel around like a helicopter while smoke billows out of the oven.

Her eyes go wide when she sees me. "Okay, I know this looks bad. But in my defense, I was left unsupervised."

I roll my lips together to keep from laughing. "What are you cooking?"

"I was trying to make my mom's lasagna. I think I left it in for too long."

"You think?" I grab an oven mitt and take the baking dish out of the oven. Tossing it into the sink, I run the water on top of it.

"We're going to starve," she whines.

"No, we won't."

"We won't?"

"Nope. We're strong independent women, remember?"

"What are we going to eat?"

"I'm going to cook. You're going to crank up the music."

"Now that I can do." Mallory skips out of the kitchen and within thirty seconds, Salt-N-Pepa are booming from my iPod speaker.

"That's what I'm talking about!" I saunter around the kitchen to the beat, gathering ingredients and mixing them together.

Mallory dances around me, setting the table and singing into a fork.

When I'm finished, I place a heaping pile of pancakes onto the table. "Scrambled eggs are up next."

"You are the perfect roommate."

"You bet your ass I am."

"Carla Evans. Did you just curse?"

I giggle. "I guess TJ's rubbing off on me."

"Please, tell me more about how he's rubbing on you." She wiggles her eyebrows and shoves a forkful of pancakes into her mouth.

"How is it that you manage to turn everything into a sexual innuendo?"

"It's a gift."

I shake my head. "He's my boss. There's no rubbing."

"You've been working some late hours. You mean to tell me you've *actually* been working?"

"He needs help. He's running that gym all by himself, and it's doing well. I want to help him so that it runs smoothly." I hold my finger up. "And please—don't say anything sexual using the word *smooth*."

Mallory pretends to zipper her lips. "Have you thought more about the yoga class?"

"I just don't feel like I'm qualified to teach it. I can follow along and do the moves, but lead a room full of people?" I shake my head. "I don't think so."

"But you're great at it. You taught me how to do that move. What's it called? Doggy style?"

A laugh bursts from my throat. "Downward-facing dog."

"Whatever. I need to get laid."

"You really do."

"Let's go find some guys tonight!"

I groan. Walked right into that one. "Let me rephrase that: You need to get laid. I'm perfectly fine."

She points her fork at me. "You, my friend, are not fine. You're still hung up on your ex. You need to get over him and under someone else. Or on top. Whichever you prefer."

"No, thanks. I'm good."

"Girl! You don't know what you're missing. You need to get out there."

"Out where?"

"I don't know. Dickland!"

"Is that like the adult version of Disney Land?"

"Yes. So let's go."

"That's just not me." Well, it was for one night ... and *God* was that incredible. But that *cannot* happen again.

"Maybe you need to branch out of your comfort zone."

"I quit my job and moved across the country. I'm well out of my comfort zone, thank you very much."

Mallory lets out an exaggerated breath. "Fine. I'll make a deal with you. Tonight, we'll watch Netflix. But tomorrow night, we go out."

"Deal."

Her eyes light up as I stand with our plates. "Really? Wow. You're easy."

"That's what she said." I wink and head for the kitchen, leaving Mallory cackling at the table.

After a Netflix marathon of *You*, I fall face-first into my pillow. I'm about to turn off my Wi-Fi for the night when I notice a text.

TJ: I'M SORRY ABOUT EARLIER. DIDN'T MEAN TO SEND YOU RUNNING for the hills.

Me: No worries. I'm not on any hills.

TJ: Good. You'd probably end up tripping and rolling down one.

Me: You can't see me but I'm scowling at you right now.

TJ: How do you know I can't see you?

TJ: Okay, that sounded way less creepy in my head.

Me: Dude, don't freak me out. I just watched a show about a stalker on Netflix with Mal.

TJ: Totally not a stalker.

Me: You'd be way too conspicuous. Like King Kong trying to hide behind a bush.

TJ: I'm better looking than King Kong.

Me: I don't know. You're definitely not as hairy.

THREE DOTS BOUNCE ON MY SCREEN WHILE TJ TYPES HIS RESPONSE. Then, they stop. I'm flirting with my boss. I know I shouldn't be. I should say goodnight and go to sleep. Still, I can't bring myself to end the conversation yet. I hold my breath when the dots reappear.

TJ: THANK YOU FOR YOUR HELP THIS WEEK. I'M GLAD I HIRED YOU.

Me: Happy to help.

TJ: Have you thought any more about the yoga class?

Me: I'm nervous.

TJ: Don't be.

Me: Poof! You fixed me. It's a miracle. ::eye roll::

TJ: You can't see me but I'm scowling at you right now.

Me: How do you know I can't see you? ::wink::

Me: OK the wink didn't make that any less creepy.

TJ: Made it worse, if anything.

Me: I'm getting sleepy. Nighty night.

TJ: See you tomorrow.

TJ: And Carla?

Me: Yeah?

TJ: What you said meant a lot.

TJ: About Superman needing help sometimes.

Me: I meant it.

TJ: Your ex is an idiot for letting you go.

MY STOMACH FLOPS. *YOU CANNOT GET BUTTERFLIES. HE'S YOUR BOSS.* I say thanks and tell him good night. Exhaling, I roll over and drift to sleep.

I have a dream that I'm on top of the Chrysler building and TJ's climbing it with his bare hands to come rescue me.

Chapter Sixteen

THE PAST

J

EVERYTHING IS BLURRY.

There's a pounding in my head. I rub my eyes and pull myself up to a seated position.

The room is dark. Tarps hanging from the ceiling surround me, ladders and buckets scattered throughout the room. A chilly breeze blows against my skin from a broken window.

Warm wetness covers my hand as I push off the ground. White, chunky vomit. I look down and my shirt's covered in it. *The downside to heroin.*

My clean hand flies to my pocket, but it's empty. I won the fight tonight, so there should be a few hundred bucks in there. I check my other pocket. Nothing but lint.

After the fight, I fucked a hot brunette. Then she'd asked if we could shoot up together. *Sonofabitch.* She robbed me.

I tear my shirt over my head and wipe the puke from my hand and around my mouth. Once I step outside, I make my way to my favorite restaurant. Their steaks are the best, and I'm hankering for one now that my stomach is empty.

I turn the corner and walk halfway down the alley. Raising my swollen knuckles to the door, I knock. One of the bus boys opens and holds up his index finger. I lean against the bricks and wait. In a few minutes, he reopens the door and hands me a plate: one half-eaten steak with mashed potatoes and two pieces of broccoli left. Jackpot. I devour the leftovers and leave the dish on the ground in the alley. Free meals, compliments of being Bobby's friend.

"I thought that was you."

I spin around and come face to face with Reggie.

"Dumpster diving, TJ?" His tongue clicks against the roof of his mouth. "You're really living large."

"Fuck you." I shoulder past him, but he catches my wrist.

"You don't have to go down this path."

"There is no other path for me. I don't have a choice."

"Do you really believe that?"

"You don't fucking get it." I flick his fancy silk tie. "You get to wear expensive suits and dine at restaurants with linen napkins and shit. You go home to a warm bed every night. Probably have a wife and kids. You don't know shit about what it's like for people like me."

"People like you are the same as people like me. The only difference is I didn't give up when life got shitty. I kept fighting."

I laugh. "I'd love to hear this one. Please, tell me how the man in the suit and tie who owns his own business is just like the homeless kid who wakes up in a puddle of his own vomit each day."

Darkness shadows over Reggie's expression. "You make assumptions about my life based on what you see, but you didn't see my struggle. You don't know the pain I've been through. I've had to claw my way through hell to get where I am today." His voice is low, menacing, and his coal eyes glisten in the light of the moon. "I had a wife and a son. Did you catch that? *Had*. My boy was a lot like you. Sex, drugs and alcohol. If it could kill him, he'd sample it.

"I tried to get a handle on him. I tried to help. But he didn't want my help. Everything I did only pushed him further away. We fought all the time. I didn't have the heart to kick him out though. I thought that would only solidify his fate. And you don't give up on family, you know?"

No, I wouldn't know anything about that. My family gave up on me a long time ago. But he's got my attention.

"One day, after I found cocaine in his room, we got into it. He took his keys and stormed out of the house. About a half-hour later, I got a call. My son had gotten into an accident. He ran a red light at a busy intersection and got into a head-on collision with a woman in a Toyota."

"What happened?"

"He went through the windshield, wasn't wearing his seatbelt. He died before the ambulance got there. The woman he hit died on impact. At least that's what they told me." Reggie exhales and his shoulders drop. "My wife drove a Toyota."

My stomach clenches and I feel like I'm going to throw up again.

"I didn't put two and two together at first. I was too busy driving to the scene of the accident and trying to get a hold of my wife. She should've been on her way home from work but she wasn't answering her cell." His voice shakes. "When I finally got through the crowd, I recognized her car."

Something cracks open inside me. Wide open. All my emotions flood me at once. His son killed his own mother. And it was an accident. A senseless accident. All because a kid made a mistake.

"So that's why you want to help me," I say. "Because you couldn't save your son."

"Everything happens for a reason. Those reasons don't always get revealed to us. But you were in my office and we crossed paths for a reason. Maybe I'm crazy for trying to help a stranger, but I'd feel crazy if I *didn't* try." Reggie grips my shoulder. "I know I can help you. I know it. All you need to do is try."

Chapter Seventeen

THE PRESENT

arla

"Hey, Ron."

"Good Morning, sweets. How you doin' today?"

I giggle. "I'm great. How you doin'?"

Ron slaps a stack of mail on the countertop and adjusts his mailbag. "You gotta put more emphasis on the *doin'*."

"I really thought I had it that time. I'll keep practicing."

He winks. "See you Monday, sweets."

I take the mail into TJ's office and set it down on his desk. The letter on top of the pile catches my eye: *New York City Department of Corrections.* It's addressed to Thomas J. Cutler.

A letter from prison?

Is TJ's name Thomas?

"Carla?"

I jump at least an inch off the ground before scurrying out from behind TJ's desk. "In your office," I call.

TJ leans against the doorjamb, his eyes scanning down my body and back up.

"Mail just came. It's on your desk." *Totally didn't snoop through it.*

"You're wearing jeans."

"Sneakers too."

"Sporty looks good on you. Kinda miss the heels though." He winks and brushes past me into his office.

I turn away to hide my pink-tinged cheeks.

"Oh, Carla. You forgot this the other night." TJ's waving my notebook overhead when I turn back around.

"Ah, that's where I left it. Thanks."

The hint of a smirk dances on his lips when I take the book from him. "Your Plan B looks great."

My jaw falls open. "You read my journal?"

"I didn't know it was yours. I opened it to check for a name."

"Then how did you know it was mine?"

"You're the only person I know who'd plan out ways to be spontaneous."

My shoulders slump. "Pretty lame, huh?"

"Hey, I never said it was lame. I can help you with everything on that list, you know."

"Really?"

"I've been wanting to go sky diving myself. And I can get you an appointment with my tattoo guy when you figure out what you want."

"I don't know if I'm ready for all that yet."

"If you wait until you feel ready, you'll never do it. That's the whole point of being spontaneous." He glances at the envelope on top of the pile and tosses it into the garbage.

"Why'd you throw that letter out? You didn't even open it." This might be overstepping but my curiosity tends to get the best of me.

"Don't need to."

"Is that what the 'T' in your name stands for? Thomas?"

He flinches at the sound of his name before nodding. "Nobody calls me that."

"What does the 'J' stand for?"

"James." He continues sifting through his mail and doesn't look at me.

"Thomas James. That's a nice name. You don't like it?"

"Nope."

"Who's sending you letters from jail?"

TJ slams his fist on the desk and my body jolts. "It's none of your business, so get back to work."

"Sorry," I mutter as I spin on my heels and close the door behind me.

TJ is always so even-keeled, I didn't expect a reaction like that. I definitely landed on a sore subject. *Note to self, don't ask your boss personal questions.*

The rest of the afternoon goes by with TJ in his office. I take messages for him and compile them onto a pad before I clock out. Walking past his door, my chest tightens. Is he okay? I lift a hand to knock but think better of it.

Like he said, *it's none of my business.*

———

THE NEXT DAY, I ARRIVE AT WORK TEN MINUTES EARLY. ROGER steps out of TJ's office and closes the door behind him.

He whistles low. "He's in a mood today."

"Again?" I ask, planting my purse under the counter.

"What do you mean again? He seemed fine when I left yesterday."

"I might've seen a piece of mail with his full name on it and asked him about it. Apparently that's off-limits." My fingers toy with the hem of my shirt. Should I ask Roger about who the letter was from?

Roger nods. "He doesn't like his name."

"Do you know why?"

"Nope. The dude is very private. He helps everyone with their shit, but nobody knows his." He shrugs.

"How's your wife feeling?" Better to change the subject. It feels wrong talking about TJ, especially when he's several feet away in the next room.

"Tired and craving sugar. I'm off to pick up three different pints of ice cream for her." He grins and shakes his head. "I can't wait to find out the sex of the baby."

My smile is genuine, though it's laced with sadness. "Your family is so blessed."

"That we are." Roger high-fives me on his way out.

I don't know how long I stand there, unmoving, like I'm cemented to the ground. I wonder what the sex of my baby would've been. So many times, I'd imagined a little girl with my dark hair, or a chubby boy with Joe's eyes. How different my life would be right now. I'd be in my second trimester.

"You okay?" TJ's touch on my shoulder snaps me out of my daze.

"Fine, why?"

"You're holding your stomach. You're not sick, are you?"

I shake my head and let my hand fall. There's nothing in there to hold on to.

Nothing but emptiness.

"You left last night before I could apologize."

I wave a hand. "It's fine."

"No, it's not. I'm sorry for snapping on you. It's not your fault and I shouldn't have spoken to you that way."

"I'm sorry too. I shouldn't have pried about your personal life."

He rubs the back of his neck. "It's just a touchy subject for me."

"Maybe you can tell me about it someday."

"Yeah, maybe. Do you have plans next weekend?"

"Just studying."

"Perfect."

My eyebrow arches. "Why?"

He struts toward the free weights and flashes me a grin over his shoulder.

I hold my hands out. "You can't leave me hanging like that!"

The bell smacks against the door as it opens and closes. The young girl from last week—the recovering addict—greets me with a smile. Her hair is slicked back in a ponytail, and her eyes are clear and bright. She looks healthy. Alive. Happy. A far cry from her disheveled appearance the last time I saw her.

"Hi. I'm here for my appointment with TJ," she says.

"What's your name? I'll let him know you're here."

"Everyone calls me Kimmie."

I walk over to where TJ is bicep-curling by the mirror. It takes everything in me not to stare at his rippling muscles, the way they stretch and contract with each movement.

I clear my throat and keep my gaze fixed on my shoes. "Kimmie's here for your session."

The metal bar clanks on the ground as TJ sets it down. "Tell her to give me a minute. Thanks."

Beads of sweat trickle down his neck and my eyes follow them until they disappear underneath the neckline of his shirt. When I realize I'm staring at him—and he's watching me with that damn smirk on his face—I whirl around and trip over a dumbbell.

TJ chuckles as he grasps my elbow and steadies me. "My bad. I shouldn't have left those there."

I point at the sign taped to the mirror that reads: Rerack your weights after each use. "You should follow your own rules."

"And you should watch where you're going instead of staring at me."

"I was not staring at you," I huff out before stomping away. I'm acting ridiculous. It's just a nice body. A perfect body, actually. The right amount of muscle, not too big, not too lean. Everything is in proportion. Everything. Even down to his—*no. Get it together.*

I smile as I approach Kimmie at the desk. "He'll be over in a sec."

"Cool. You're new here, right?"

"Yep. I'm Carla."

"How do you know TJ?"

"I ... uh ... Through friends. What about you?"

"Met him at an NA meeting."

"Don't you mean AA?"

"Alcoholics go to Alcoholics Anonymous. Drug addicts go to Narcotics Anonymous."

My brows lift. "Oh. Okay." *Why would he go there if he had a drinking problem?*

"I'm pretty open about my addiction. TJ says it helps to be upfront about it. Don't be ashamed of something that's a part of who you are. It helps you take control of it instead of letting it control you."

"Sounds like smart advice."

"TJ's the best. He's such an inspiration after everything he's been through."

I nod, wondering what exactly happened in his past. My eyes find him across the gym. "It's hard to imagine him any less perfect than he is now."

"You like him."

"Is there anyone who doesn't?" I busy myself filing papers so as not to make eye contact with the perceptive teenager.

"Ready, Kimmie cakes?" TJ calls as he struts over to us.

She groans. "That's the worst one yet."

"What's wrong with that nickname?" TJ asks. "It's cute."

I shake my head. "Cute is the exact opposite of what a teenage girl wants to be called."

"Thank you!" Kimmie fist-bumps me and follows TJ.

For the next hour, I'm entranced by the way TJ interacts with Kimmie. He pushes her to train hard and doesn't hold back. He doesn't treat her differently because she's young, or because she's a girl. She tires easily and asks to quit several times, but he doesn't let up. At the end of her session, they sit facing each other on the mat and TJ does quite a bit of talking.

"Carla." He's waving me over.

"What's up?"

"Why don't you join us? I think Kimmie can use some of your wisdom."

My eyebrows fly to my hairline. "Me? Oh, no. I don't think I have much wisdom to share."

"Come on," Kimmie pleads. "TJ's great and all, but I need some girl power right now."

I climb the stairs and duck under the ropes, taking a seat beside Kimmie. "What's going on?"

"I don't really have a lot of girl friends," she says. "And I can't talk to my mom about this stuff."

"Ah, this sounds like boy stuff."

She nods. "How do you know if a guy likes you?"

"Well, that's kind of different for every guy. Some guys are more straight-forward. Others are too shy to make a move. Who is the boy in question?"

Kimmie's cheeks turn pink. "His name is Tyler. He's my best friend. Sometimes I think he's flirting with me, but other times I think he looks at me like one of the guys. I don't want to ruin the friendship, but maybe it would be great if we could be more than friends. I just don't know what to do. I'm not pretty and confident like you."

I choke out a laugh. "I am not that confident. I second-guess myself all the time. And you are pretty, Kimmie. You just don't see that yet. You need to appreciate and love the person you are. Don't put yourself down and don't sell yourself short."

"Easy for you to say."

TJ opens his mouth but I hold my finger up. "Look at you in here. You didn't give up. You're fighting. I admire you for doing this. You're so young, yet you're stronger than so many people older than you. You should be proud of yourself. Any guy would be lucky to date you. And if it's not Tyler, there will be plenty more. Trust me."

Tears brim and streak down her cheeks. "Nobody's ever said that about me before."

"Nobody has to for you to believe it, kiddo." TJ places his hand on her shoulder. "Don't wait for other people to tell you how great you are. Start telling yourself that every day."

As we're walking toward the front desk and saying goodbye to Kimmie, the phone rings. I jog around the counter. "Thanks for calling Heavy Weight. How can I help you?"

The line clicks before a recording plays. "This is a call from the New York City Department of Corrections. Please press zero to accept this call."

Uh-oh. My body tenses and my eyes flick to TJ.

"Everything okay?" he mouths.

"Uh ..." I lower my voice and say, "It's the Department of Corrections."

TJ stalks behind the counter, takes the receiver from my hand, and slams it down. "Never accept that call. Got it?"

I swallow. "Got it."

"I'll be in my office if you need me."

First the letter, and now the phone call.

Who's trying to contact him from prison?

Chapter Eighteen

THE PAST

REGGIE'S APARTMENT IS SWEET.

Well, he has a king-sized bed and his fridge is stocked with food. That's about as far as I've gotten. What more do I need to see?

"Here's the living room. There's the kitchen. Bathroom's down the hall by my bedroom. I don't keep any money here and I don't own anything valuable, so there's nothing for you to steal."

I open my mouth to respond but he stops me with a raised hand.

"You're going to go through withdrawals. It's going to be ugly and you're going to feel like you're dying. You'll get desperate. There's nothing more dangerous than an addict who's detoxing."

"You make it sound so fun."

"I'll never bullshit you. All I ask is that you don't bullshit me."

I nod.

"There's clean towels in the bathroom. Go take a shower. You're filthy and you smell like garbage." Reggie turns and disappears into the kitchen.

Under the hot spray of the shower, I scrub my skin until it's raw.

No matter how many times I lather myself in soap, I never feel clean enough. I suppose it's because I can't wash the memories away. They're forever burned into my skin like tattoos.

When I think about the events that led me here, it's as if I'm watching someone else's life play out. I was a good kid. I had a semi-normal life—lots of kids grow up with alcoholic parents and they end up just fine. Mom and I dealt with Dad as best as we could. I had friends. I got decent grades. I had a home. How did I end up *here*?

An addict.

Homeless.

What could I have done differently? I spend a long time searching for that answer, until tears sting my eyes. It's a weird sensation. I haven't cried since I watched Mom die. Maybe I'm crying now because I'm finally getting the help I need. Or maybe I'm terrified about the future and what's to come. Nothing good has ever happened to me. How can I trust that this next phase will be any different?

I curl into a ball on the floor of the tub, the sobs racking my body.

I can't do this. I'm not strong enough.

I have to do this. I don't have any other options.

They say it doesn't matter if you lose the battle as long as you win the war. I've lost many of the battles in my life. But this feels different. This feels bigger. I guess it's time I prepare for war.

Chapter Nineteen

THE PRESENT

arla

I WRAP MALLORY'S CARDIGAN AROUND MY MIDSECTION AND TIE THE straps in a tight bow. As much as I'm loving the gorgeous colors of October in New York, I'm not prepared for the chilly temperatures. Mental note: I need a new wardrobe.

The gym door opens and I shiver again.

"Hi. I'm here to see TJ. My name is Sam."

"Hi, Sam. Let me get him for you." I rap my knuckles against TJ's office door and peek my head inside.

Oh, holy hell. He's sitting at his desk, writing in a notebook, wearing the sexiest pair of black-framed glasses. Forget Superman. Hello, Clark Kent.

"I didn't know you wear glasses."

"I told you I'm getting old."

I laugh. "Sam's here to see you."

He slides his glasses off and sets them on the desk. "It's been a while since I've written in a journal," he says, closing the notebook. "You inspired me to start writing again."

"What made you stop?"

His shoulders lift. "Life."

Right. Vague, one-word answers. Must be Tuesday.

I help Sam fill out his paperwork while TJ sets up their equipment.

Sam looks like a regular gym-goer. In his twenties. Decent build. But when I look closer, I notice he's a bit different.

His eyes blink more often than everyone else's. His eyebrows repetitively pinch together while he's speaking. The muscles in his arms contract as he clenches his fists over and over again. Sometimes, he'll make a sound like something's stuck in his throat and he has to keep clearing it.

When he's sparring with TJ, you'd never see it. His body is busy and his mind is concentrating on the task at hand. It's when he takes a break, or talks. That's when it happens.

Toward the end of each of TJ's sessions, he sits in the middle of the ring with his clients and talks to them. They hang on to his every word. I can't blame them. I'm enamored by his commanding presence even when he's just talking about the weather.

I start by racking the dumbbells, my ears straining to catch snippets of their conversation. Then I walk around the ring, taking the long way to the opposite side of the gym to clean the mirrors. When I circle back, I'm caught.

"Vulture or shark?" TJ calls.

My spine stiffens and my nose scrunches. "Huh?"

"Sam here wants to know why the pretty girl is circling us like a vulture. I told him you remind me more of a shark. So, which one is it?"

My cheeks flame. "I'm sorry, Sam. Didn't mean to interrupt your session."

Sam's fist knocks against his leg several times as he smiles. "That's okay," he says, clearing his throat. "You're much easier on the eyes than this guy. Couldn't help myself."

TJ chuckles. "Not gonna argue with you on that."

I lean my elbows onto the mat outside the ring and smile. "How did you like your first session?"

"I loved it. I really think it's going to help me."

"Sam has Tourette's," TJ says. "Studies have shown that exercise can lessen the severity of his tics."

"Tics?"

"My body performs these frequent movements," Sam says. "Kind of like constant twitches."

"And you can't stop them?"

He shakes his head. "They're involuntary. They get worse as my emotions heighten."

"Like if you're nervous or excited?"

"Exactly."

I frown. "That must be hard."

"Was made fun of every day growing up. Even my dad didn't understand it. People still stare at me like I'm a freak."

"You're not a freak. They're the freaks for being so rude."

TJ claps Sam on the back. "Now he's taking control of his life and learning how to rise above all those judgmental pricks."

"You're in good hands." I offer Sam a reassuring smile and a wave before heading back to work.

Twenty minutes later, TJ's saying goodbye to Sam and walking him to the door. He comes around the desk and hovers too close to where I stand, leaning his hip against the counter beside me. "Sam's smitten with you."

I laugh and shake my head. "He's sweet."

"I want you to teach that yoga class. You'd be great at it."

"How do you know? I could be horrible at yoga and you'd have no idea."

He grins like he's won. "You're right. So teach me and I'll see for myself."

"You want me to teach you how to do yoga?"

"Yes. Tonight."

———

"Now breathe in through your nose. Allow your stomach to expand as it fills with oxygen. Focus on your breathing. Keep your chin up. Shoulders down away from your ears."

"How am I supposed to keep my shoulders down when my arms are up over my head?" TJ asks, cracking one eye open.

"Watch me." I raise my arms straight above me and drop my shoulders. "Your shoulders are tight. That's where you carry your stress. Try to be conscious of how you're carrying yourself."

"You're very observant."

"Yoga taught me to be more aware of my body's reaction to stress. Once you catch it, you can correct it."

"Shoulders down. Got it. What's next?"

"Open your arms like this, and swivel on your back leg."

TJ swivels but loses his balance. His thick arms flail as he tries to regain his stance. "Almost got it."

My teeth dig into my bottom lip. "You okay?"

"Pfft. I'm fine. I'm a natural."

I step closer to him and adjust the position of his leg. Then I place my hands on his waist to tilt his body. "Keep your arms out, wide and straight."

His gaze weighs on me but I don't dare look up when we're this close. His stomach muscles clench under my fingers and it takes all the strength in me to keep them from roaming over his sculpted body.

"Keep breathing," I say, though it's more for my sake than his.

"What's this move called?" His breath dances along my skin, lips inches away.

"Warrior Two. This one's my favorite."

"Why's that?"

"It makes me feel strong."

"You *are* strong. And you could help other people find their strength with this class."

"How did you become so strong?"

"Why do you always ask so many questions?"

"Maybe it's because you answer every question with another question."

"Maybe I don't like to talk about my past."

"Maybe that's your problem."

"I have a problem? Didn't realize. Good thing you're here to tell me."

"Yeah, good thing. Otherwise you might not have anyone in your life with enough balls to tell you what a hypocrite you're being."

His arms cross over his chest and I know I've struck a nerve. "How am I a hypocrite?"

"You want me to open up to you about all my problems, yet you snap at me whenever I ask something about you. You help all these people who come in here and make them bare their souls to you, but God forbid you do the same. Maybe you're the one who needs a good training session. Practice what you preach."

TJ's jaw works under his skin. He's quiet and I lose all hope of getting a response ... until he speaks. "You're right."

"Really?" I clear my throat. "I mean, yes. Of course I am."

"What do you want to know?"

"We don't have to do this right now."

"Come on. Now's your chance." He lowers himself to the floor and sits, patting the space next to him.

"Fine." I sit facing him. "Who's trying to contact you from jail?"

"My dad."

"What does he want?"

"Don't know, don't care."

"You aren't curious?"

"There's nothing he could say that I'd want to hear."

"What did he do ... to get put in prison?"

He lets out a long exhale. "He committed second-degree murder."

Wow. Wasn't expecting that. "When was the last time you saw him?"

"The day the police took him away in handcuffs. Twelve years ago."

"Has he tried to reach out to you before?"

"No."

"So why now, after all this time?"

"Like I said before: Don't know, don't care."

Silence settles between us, though my mind is loud and chaotic.

"Feel better now?" he asks.

"Not exactly, no. But this isn't about making me feel better. This is about you. You're so closed off. Your dad committed a crime, yet you're the one who's acting like you're locked up because of it. It's not right."

"You don't know what my life has been like."

"What about where your life is going? What about the future? You're the one who told me I need to live in the present, yet here you are letting your past dictate the way your life turns out."

He shakes his head. "I'm good where I'm at right now. My future? This is it for me. Don't try to make this anything more."

I tried to crack open the door to TJ's life, but he just slammed it in my face. I might've learned about a piece of his past, yet it only makes things more confusing.

I remain where I am while I watch him stand and walk out of the room.

Chapter Twenty
THE PAST

I AM GOING TO DIE.

I'm dying. That's what's happening. The pain ripping through my insides. The violent vomiting. The shaking and the sweating and the not sleeping. This has to be what death feels like.

"Are you sure no one's ever died from this?" My voice sounds like I swallowed a sheet of sandpaper and washed it down with a dozen razorblades.

Reggie sighs. "Like I've told you the past twenty times: You're not going to die."

I groan and roll onto my side. It's been one week since I shot up. Seven days since I've had a drink. Withdrawal is pure torture. Reggie says it gets worse before it gets better. I sure as fuck hope this is the *worse* part.

He wasn't kidding when he said I'd get desperate. I've taken a few swings at him—landed one. I attempted to sneak out while he was asleep—he wasn't. Last night, I even thought about stabbing him in the leg with his own kitchen knife during dinner.

It's crazy how the mind succumbs to the addiction. You crave the drug the way your lungs crave oxygen. The pain of withdrawal is so intense, all you want is the very thing that put you in this situation just to make it stop.

"You're almost out of the woods." Reggie drapes a cold washcloth over my forehead.

"I'm going to die in these woods."

"You'll need to remember this when you feel the itch to use again."

"Once it's out of my system, won't the cravings stop?"

Reggie pins me with a look. "The cravings will never stop. It's in you. You're going to fight this for the rest of your life."

"Then what's the fucking point?"

"That is the point. If you can do this, you can do anything. You'll be stronger. Smarter. Better." The corner of the bed lifts as he stands. "And you won't be dead."

You're going to fight this for the rest of your life. My stomach rolls and I reach for the bucket.

Chapter Twenty-One

THE PRESENT

arla

"You can't be serious!"

"Why not?" TJ taps my notebook. "It's on your list."

"Because ... this is expensive. And I don't have the money to pay you back right now."

"You don't need to pay me back."

I hold the sky diving pamphlet in front of his face. "This isn't something you can spring on me. I need to ... I ..."

"You want to live in the moment more, don't you?"

"Yes, but—"

"And you want to go sky diving, don't you?"

"Yes, but—"

"Then we're going. End of discussion." TJ swivels and waltzes toward the door. He holds it open with his foot and curls his index finger at me. "Let's go, baby doll."

My heart races and my palms are slick with sweat as I ball them at my sides. "TJ, this is insane."

"The fact that I paid for you, or the fact that we're about to jump out of a perfectly good airplane?"

"Both."

"Consider the money a bonus."

"For what? I've only been working a few weeks."

He sighs and rubs the stubble on his jawline. "Can we argue about this in my truck? I don't want to miss our jump time."

My hands tremble. "I'm not ready for this yet. I needed to work up to this. It's scary, not to mention how expensive it is. I just wrote that list in my notebook on a whim. I didn't actually mean to complete it right now. It's more of a bucket list. Something I do over a span of time, you know? And—hey!"

TJ hoists me over his shoulder and strides out into the parking lot. "We'll never make it if you keep naming all the reasons you shouldn't. Don't get your panties in a bunch."

"My panties are not bunched! Put me down," I shout, flailing to get out of his grip.

TJ swings open his passenger door and I bounce onto the seat when he flings me inside. I smooth my hair down, chest heaving. "This is kidnapping, you know."

He laughs as he shuts the door and jogs around to the driver's side. His amusement only infuriates me further.

When he pulls out of the parking lot, my heart sinks into my stomach. *I'm really going sky diving.*

Twenty minutes into the trip, TJ glances at me. "Are you going to give me the silent treatment the entire ride?"

My arms are crossed and I'm facing away from him.

"Carla, it's just money."

I say nothing.

"The real reason you're mad is because you're not in control. If you want to change, you need to push yourself to do things outside your comfort zone."

My eyes remain fixed on the trees as we whiz by, their leaves such warm, vibrant colors. Fall in Florida never looked like this.

"Wanna fuck?"

My head swivels Exorcist-style. "Excuse me?"

TJ's grinning. "Knew that'd get you to say something."

I roll my eyes.

"Tell me why you're mad."

"I'm not mad," I say with a sigh. "I'm more embarrassed than anything. I feel like your charity case. *Poor Carla. She's so rigid and needs to lighten up. I have to teach her how to have fun.*"

The truck jerks to the right and comes to an abrupt stop in the gravel on the side of the highway. TJ shifts in his seat and pins me with intensity. "You are not a charity case. I'm not doing this because I feel bad for you, nor am I doing this because I feel like I have to. I don't need to teach you how to be fun. You were fun the night we met and had incredible sex, and you were fun when all we did was shop for office supplies.

"I'm not trying to change you into someone you're not. I'm trying to help you see the woman I see in you. I'm sorry you feel forced to do this. I was only trying to help. If you want me to turn around, I'll see if I can get a refund on our jump package. I just thought it would be nice to experience this ... together."

My skin prickles at his words. "You think our sex was incredible?"

TJ's head falls back as he laughs. "Out of everything I said, that's what you heard?"

I shrug, my lips curling into a smile.

"Confession?" He picks at the steering wheel. "I think about our night together a lot."

A flush climbs my chest, rising up my throat and into my cheeks. "Why is that?"

TJ leans against his headrest, eyes closing for a moment. "Because it felt good. You felt good."

"Do you do that often? One-night stands?"

He averts his gaze out the windshield at the passing cars. "No. I stopped that a long time ago."

"Then why me?" My pulse throbs in my ears as I count the seconds until his response.

"You're stunningly beautiful. There's an attraction between us, I know you feel it." He blows a long stream of air through his nostrils. "You're so put together, so in control. But I see a wildness in your eyes when you look at me. That night, I wanted to unravel you. I wanted to watch you come undone. There's so much fire and passion inside you. You don't even know it. You should harness it. Don't let anyone stifle you."

A zing shoots straight through my heart, like a dead engine roaring to life for the first time in ages. Hot fuel courses through every valve. The air between us is electric, our bodies sparking and crackling in anticipation.

TJ stares at me, hard. *Now what?* his eyes say.

I swallow down the apprehension caught in my throat. "I don't want you to get a refund. I want to do this. With you."

His velvety lips curve up. "Then let's go."

———

I'M FREEFALLING FROM THE SKY. MY STOMACH SOMERSAULTS AS I plummet to the earth. White puffy clouds float above me, casting shadows onto the grass below. The wind rips through my hair, my skin rippling, arms and legs splayed out wide.

As terrifying as this is—no safety net to catch me, no guarantee that the parachute will open—a strange sense of calm washes over me. Up here in the atmosphere, I find peace.

We are small fragments in this world. Our problems, the things that trouble us, the things we hold on to, are all part of a bigger picture. Maybe it's because nothing seems that serious when you're faced with the possibility of death. Maybe I just needed to change my perspective. The view from up here is crystal clear.

I am going to be okay.

It can all end in a moment, and I need to make my time count for something. My baby didn't get to have a life. I owe it to him or her to live mine to the fullest.

When my feet are planted on the ground, my tandem diver unclips me. My knees drop to the grass. I gasp for air and pull my goggles off, tears sliding down my cheeks.

I am going to be okay.

TJ, who'd jumped before me, rushes to my side. "Are you all right? Did you get hurt?"

I shake my head and wipe my cheeks with the backs of my trembling hands. "I'm ... that was ... incredible."

"So those are happy tears?"

I choke out a laugh in between sobs. "Yes. Very happy."

My legs are wobbly so TJ wraps his hand around mine and helps me up. We're quiet on the way out, and for a good while on the way home, but he hasn't let my hand go. I wonder what he's thinking about. I won't ask. Jumping out of that plane was a very personal experience and I don't want to ruin it. I've asked enough questions for today.

When we pull up to the gym, TJ kills the engine. Neither of us makes a move to exit.

"Thank you," I say.

"I'm proud of you." His pinky wraps around mine on the center console.

I fixate on our arms touching. The hardness of his muscular forearm beside the softness of mine. His ink-black swirls a stark difference from my spotless skin.

I trace the pictures on his arm, my fingers skating up his wrist to the crook of his elbow. That's when I notice the scars. Four, raised, dark-purple bumps in the midst of his tattoos. Kimmie's voice connects the dots in my mind: *Met him at an NA meeting.*

TJ's breathing changes as he shifts in his seat. He tries to pull his arm away from me, but I grab on tighter. Lowering my lips to the inside of his arm, I kiss the scars from his past. His eyes squeeze shut, like it pains him to watch something so tender.

"You shouldn't feel ashamed." My fingers continue along his arm, his bicep, and around the curve of his shoulder.

His eyes open and he hits me with his heated gaze. Raw, potent. Need and desire well inside me like the surge of a storm.

I don't know who moves first or if we act at the same time, but in the blink of an eye I'm straddling him. His hands are in my hair, lips fused to mine. Our mouths open simultaneously, tongues stroking each other. Each move is deliberate and greedy. My hips rock against him and he grips my hair tighter, groaning into my mouth.

I've heard adrenaline makes you do crazy things. Is that what's coursing through me right now? Or is it something more? That thought brings a myriad of emotions, but I push every single one away. I'm living in the moment. I'll worry about my decisions later.

TJ's warm tongue slides down my neck, nipping and sucking at my skin. Just as I'm about to lift the hem of his shirt, he stops. His hands, his mouth—everything freezes. The sound of our quick breaths fill the cab of the truck. Then slowly, he pushes me back onto the passenger seat.

I wait for him to say something. Anything. He won't even look in my direction. *Did I do something wrong?* I want to ask, but I'm afraid to hear his answer.

So I let myself out of his truck, I get into my car, and I drive away.

Chapter Twenty-Two

THE PAST

~~DEAR DIARY~~,

~~Dear Journal~~,

Maybe I don't have to address this to anyone specific …

My therapist told me it might be helpful to write my thoughts and emotions in a journal. I told him it was a stupid idea. He told me he's the one getting paid six figures and so I should listen to him. The dude's funny. I like him.

Therapy isn't what I thought it would be. Reggie suggested I talk to a shrink about my childhood. By *suggested* I mean he told me I had to go. He's footing the bill, so it's not like I'm losing anything.

Reggie's also letting me crash on his couch. Since I can't pay rent, or any of the other bills, I help out at his gym. I'm answering phones, cleaning toilets, whatever he needs me to do. He's holding onto my paychecks. He said he'll let me have the money once I complete the twelve steps. Sometimes I wonder if I can trust him. The truth is, I don't really have a choice. The man gave me a place to live, got me sobered up, and he cooks for me every night. He's even teaching me how to cook. Reggie has done more for me in two months than my own father did for me in thirteen years.

I still hate going to the meetings. Reggie has me going to both Alcoholic's and Narcotic's Anonymous. It's crazy to hear some of the shit people do when they're fucked up. Some people have it a lot worse ~~than I do~~ than I did. It doesn't make me feel better, but it's interesting to see that even the executive in the Armani suit and the mom from the suburbs have something in common with me. Some of the strongest people there fall off the wagon. Yet, everyone supports them and they get back up and keep trying.

I don't know if I'll ever relapse. I sure hope not. Withdrawal was a real bitch. Felt like I was dying. Maybe I'll write a journal entry about what it felt like, so if I ever get the urge to use again, I can read it and remind myself how much it sucked.

I think I'll go do that now.

Chapter Twenty-Three

THE PRESENT

arla

I STARE AT MY PHONE, WILLING IT TO MAKE A NOISE.

No dancing dots. No response. No ring.

I sigh and scroll for Roger's number instead.

"Hello?"

"Hey, Rog. Can you explain why I'm staring at a sign on the gym door that says, *'Closed for vacation'?*"

"We're closed until Monday. You didn't know?"

I sigh again. "Wouldn't be standing here if I did."

"Ah, Carla, I'm sorry. I thought TJ told you."

"And why are we closed?"

"TJ closes this time every year. He goes on vacation."

"Vacation?" I can't help the surprise in my voice.

"He never takes off save for these same three days each year."

"Where does he go?"

A loud screeching sound, something like a cross between a pterodactyl and Godzilla, pierces my eardrum through the phone.

"Gotta go," Roger says. "Fatherhood calls."

I smile but it quickly fades. I snap a picture of the sign and send it to TJ in a text that says, *Thanks for the heads up.*

Today makes five days since the abruptly-stopped make-out session in TJ's truck. During those five days, he avoided me with the skill of an experienced CIA agent. I've racked my brain to pinpoint what happened that day.

Was it me? Did I misread his signals? I distinctly remember him kissing me back. I jumped on top of him like a spider monkey in heat ... maybe I was too aggressive?

Whatever his reason is for giving me the silent treatment this week, it's not an excuse to treat me like I don't exist.

Maybe I should look for another job.

———

"THIS IS THE LAST ONE." I GRUNT AS I PLOP THE BOX ONTO THE floor.

"Thanks so much for helping," Charlotte says.

I bounce onto her bed. "That's what friends are for."

Mallory saunters through the doorway holding three glasses of wine. "No, *this* is what friends are for." We each take one and she raises hers in the air. "Congrats on moving in with your hunk of a man. Now you get to have loud monkey sex whenever you want."

Charlotte's horrified expression coupled with Tanner's laughter in the other room paints a satisfied smirk on Mallory's face.

I wrap my arm around Charlotte. "My little girl is all grown up. Remember the days when we wanted to marry Jess and Dean?"

"I still want to marry Jess," she says.

"I heard that!" Tanner yells.

"I love you, babe!"

Mallory raises an eyebrow at me. "Wouldn't have pegged you for a Dean gal."

"Five words." I hold up my fingers and count. "He built her a car."

"He was too whiny for me. Logan was the best one for Rory."

I roll my eyes. "He's a cheater. You're right. Great catch."

"He only cheats on his girl because he's in love with Rory."

"And that makes it so much better."

We continue to drink while we discuss the fictional boys of *Gilmore Girls*. On our third glasses, we decide it's time to start unpacking.

Charlotte nudges me with her shoulder. "Have you talked to Joe?"

I shake my head. "But he still calls and texts. The man is persistent, I'll give him that."

"Are you ever going to tell me what happened with you guys?"

The hurt in her eyes pulls at the guilt in my stomach, which is now sloshing around in a sea of wine. My defenses are weakened. I guess it's time to tell her. So I stare up at the ceiling and tell her everything.

Charlotte gasps when I finish. "You were pregnant?"

The news shocks Mallory into silence, a feat in itself.

"I was, for two and a half months."

Charlotte flings her arms around my shoulders, sniffling in my hair. "I'm so sorry I wasn't there when you needed me."

"It's not your fault. You were busy being kidnapped by psychopaths."

"That piece of shit broke up with you because you were pregnant? That douchebag deserves to have his balls cut off!" And Mal's back.

"That's why you moved here," Charlotte says. "To get away."

I nod and gulp down the remainder of my wine. "I planned our future for over four years. It was the only plan I had. Starting over in a new place just made sense. Plan A didn't work out, so I had to come up with Plan B." Pain slices through my chest. *Where the hell is TJ?*

"My sister had a miscarriage in between my niece and nephew. She cried for a long time. Didn't get out of bed for a month." Mallory pours more wine into my glass, finishing off the bottle. "It's heartwrenching when you lose a baby like that."

"How did she get through it?"

"Time."

I face-plant into a pillow and groan.

"Everything happens for a reason," Charlotte says. She rubs her hand in small circles on my back. "I know it's cliché, but it's true. It's God's way of telling you that Joe wasn't the right one for you."

"Couldn't God have sent me a postcard instead?" I mutter.

Mallory clears her throat. "Dear Carla, Greetings from Heaven. Joe is a smelly asshole. I'm gonna need you to break up with him. I'll send you someone else soon. XOXO God."

I chuckle, pushing off the pillow to sit up. "What about you, Mal? How's your love life?"

Charlotte pokes her ribs. "Yeah, whatever happened with that guy who gave you his number at the bakery the other night?"

Mallory grimaces and covers her eyes with her hands. "He sent me a dick pic!"

Charlotte and I groan in unison.

"Are you kidding me? Sal? The guy who comes in every night to get a coffee and flirt with you?"

Mal nods. "Yup. Him. Want to see his penis?"

"No!" we shout.

"You know, I don't understand men. You want to get a girl to like you? Don't send a dick pic. I already know you have a dick. I don't need to see a picture of it. What they should send is a picture of them cooking dinner. Washing the dishes. Doing laundry. Or even a pic of them doing their taxes. Something useful. Something that will show me you are a functional human being who's capable of taking care of himself."

"Yes!" I high-five her. "We should start our own dating app. Forget Tinder."

Mallory's eyes light up. "That's actually an awesome idea."

The rest of the day is spent just like this. Tanner orders pizza for us. Mallory hits on the delivery guy. None of Charlotte's things get unpacked.

And I laugh so hard, my stomach muscles ache.

———

Monday afternoon, I'm a ball of nerves.

I check my reflection in the rearview mirror one last time before heading into the gym for my shift. I spot TJ's truck parked a few spots over. My chest tightens. Good. At least he's alive.

Inside, TJ's behind the counter talking with Roger. When his eyes meet mine, without missing a beat, he smiles.

He *smiles*.

I don't know what I was expecting, but none of the scenarios I created in my head prepared me for this.

Roger gives me a nod and a wave on his way out. TJ and I are left facing each other behind the desk.

"Hi," he says.

I slam my purse down. "Hi? That's what you have to say to me?"

"Look, I know I have a lot of explaining to do, but—"

"No." I poke his chest with my index finger, and try not to wince. It's like poking steel. "You don't have to explain anything to me. *It's none of my business*, remember?" I press into him again. "You want to kiss me and then ignore me for a week? Whatever. You want to disappear for three days? Go ahead. But if you think I'm not getting compensated for those days when you failed to mention we were closing, you'd better think again!"

I spent a good part of the weekend planning out what I wanted to say when I saw him. This isn't what I practiced.

His lips twitch and there's a glint in his eyes. "That's what you're angry about? You want to get paid for the past three days?"

I cross my arms over my chest. "That's at the top of my list, yes."

"Please tell me you actually wrote a list of reasons why you're mad at me, and that you'll let me read it."

"It's in my head. You're missing the point."

"Yes, Carla. I will pay you for the days you had off."

I give him a curt nod and turn around, trying to make myself look busy—but all I'm doing is moving folders from one side of the counter to the other.

His hands on my hips and his warm breath in my ear stills my entire body. "Have dinner with me tonight. I'll explain everything."

I want to tell him I don't care to hear what he has to say.

I want to tell him I have plans tonight.

I want to tell him to stop touching me.

But I do care, and I don't have plans.

And I definitely don't want him to stop touching me.

Chapter Twenty-Four
THE PAST

J

"WAKE UP!"

My body jolts upright, fist swinging out in front of me.

Reggie dodges my blind punch. "One of these nights, you're going to clip me."

"Shit," I mumble, rubbing the blurriness from my eyes.

"Same nightmare?"

"Same one."

"Write it down," he says as he stands. "Shrinks love to analyze dreams."

I flop back onto the bed, heart slowing to a canter. "I'm sorry for waking you again."

"Wouldn't wake me if you had your own apartment."

"We've been over this, Reg. I'm not ready for that yet."

"You won't be if you keep telling yourself that."

I thrust my hand through my damp hair. "What if I'm tempted and you're not there?"

"Then you call me. You think every sponsor lives with his sponsee?"

"I just don't think I'm ready. I need some more time."

"I think you're scared. You're in your head too much. You're not letting yourself recover because you're stuck in the past. That's what these dreams are all about."

"Maybe I don't need to keep going to therapy. Got my own personal shrink right here at home."

"Don't put that shit on me." His tone is harsh, but his eyes dance with amusement. "I wear enough hats as it is. Next you'll be wanting me to wipe your ass."

A smirk pulls at the corner of my mouth. "Don't act like you don't wanna see my ass, Reg."

"Why do you think I've been having you do all those squats?" He pauses in the doorway, leaning a shoulder against the frame. His smile falters. "I won't be here forever, TJ. You've got to be ready to take care of yourself. Live the second chance at life you've been given."

"I'm living it."

"Sleeping on an old man's couch, working, and watching Jeopardy every night ain't living. There's more out there for you. Don't be afraid to reach out and take it. You've earned it."

"You'd miss me too much."

"Joke all you want, but the truth still remains." His index finger is pointing straight at me. "Don't punish yourself for the sins of your father."

Chapter Twenty-Five
THE PRESENT

arla

"YOU READY?"

"Just let me clean the counter."

"Leave it. Come on. It's after seven." TJ takes the cleaning spray from my hand and sets it on the counter.

"Fine, but don't blame me when everyone contracts the flu virus because I didn't sanitize the front desk."

I follow him up the stairs leading to his apartment. I don't know if I'm nervous about what he's going to tell me, or because of the things we did the last time I was in his apartment. Let's go with both.

"What do you feel like having for dinner?" he asks.

"Tacos."

He lifts an eyebrow. "You like Mexican food?"

"Whenever I'm given a choice, the answer is always tacos."

"Tacos it is."

I kick off my heels and flop onto the couch while TJ places our order.

"It reclines," he whispers.

My eyes widen and my fingers fumble around for the button on the armrest. I close my eyes and smile while my body tilts back.

"Food will be here in about forty minutes," TJ says, taking the seat beside me. "Comfy?"

"In Heaven, there will be tacos and this chair."

He chuckles.

I sit upright and face him, crossing my legs. "So, what is it that you wanted to tell me?"

He clears his throat and runs a hand through his hair. I watch as his chest rises and falls with each of his deep breaths. I wait, allowing him time to collect his thoughts. Whatever he's about to tell me seems important.

"Saturday was my birthday ... and the anniversary of my mom's death."

My eyebrows lift. "Your mom died on your birthday?"

"Yep. Gives Happy Birthday a whole new meaning, huh?" He laughs once. "So every year on my birthday, I drive to New Jersey and spend a few days there. I couldn't afford to have a funeral for Mom when she died, so the state cremated her body. Woods drove me to the beach so I could throw her ashes into the water. She always wanted to go to the beach, but Dad never wanted to take us. I figured that's where she'd want to be."

"Who's Woods?"

"He was a friend. Sort of. My dad used to hit my mom whenever he was drunk. I had to call the police a lot, and Woods was the officer who always came. He tried to help me from time to time while I was in and out of foster care."

"Do you still talk to him?"

"Not since I was sixteen. The night he released me from jail." TJ turns his head to look at me for the first time since we started this conversation. Shame fills his eyes. "I wasn't always this person you see now."

Any anger I had left melts away. I lift my hand to caress his cheek, and he leans into my touch. I want to climb in his lap and wrap my arms around him. I want to hold him and tell him how sorry I am. But

I know that won't change anything. Words won't take his pain away. *Don't I know it.*

"Thank you for sharing that with me," I whisper.

"When you told me I need to practice what I preach, it really hit home."

"TJ, I'm sorry I said that. I didn't know—"

"No. You were right. My friend Reggie used to tell me how important it is to talk about the things I went through. He said I isolate myself."

"Do you remember what I asked you the night we met?"

One corner of his mouth turns up. "You asked me why I was torturing myself."

I nod. "You can't punish yourself for the life you were given. You can't go back and change anything. Look at the person you are now."

TJ's chin drops and he averts his eyes.

"No." I grip his face and turn it back towards me. "You are an incredible man. You should be proud of the life you've made for yourself. You devote your life to helping others. Take some time to help yourself."

"How do I do that?"

"You need to learn to love yourself. You told me love wasn't meant for you, but you're wrong."

"And how do you know that?"

"Because love doesn't discriminate. Love is meant for everyone."

He falls silent again, undoubtedly wrestling with his demons.

"Well, you're off the hook for closing the gym without telling me," I say.

"For the record, I'm really sorry about that." TJ scrubs a hand over his jaw. "And about what happened after sky diving."

"Sorry like you regret it, or ..." My voice trails off because I don't know what else to say without sounding like a needy chick.

"Is that what you've been thinking this whole time? That I regretted kissing you?"

I shrug. "Girl kisses boy. Boy pushes girl away and says nothing. Then boy ignores girl and disappears for three days. There the conclusions were. I didn't have to jump far."

"With the anniversary of my mom's death, my head wasn't in a good space. A lot of old shit gets dug up. I didn't want to drag you into my mess of emotions. Didn't want to take advantage of the situation. Of you."

"So, what you're saying is ..."

"No, I did not regret the kiss. And if I'm being honest, I wanted to keep going."

My eyes land on his lips, heart hammering in my chest. "I like when you're honest."

TJ edges forward, tucking a strand of hair behind my ear. My heart stalls, breath faltering. All logic and reasoning fly out the window when we're this close.

Three solid knocks on the door bring me back down to earth.

I've never been so unhappy to see tacos in my life.

While we're eating, I summon the courage to ask another personal question. "Have you ever gone to visit your dad in jail?"

TJ shakes his head and swallows. "I've never wanted to. He doesn't deserve a visitor."

"I get it. I wouldn't want to see him either."

He arches a brow. "You're not going to lecture me about not going?"

"Why would I? I don't blame you for not wanting to see him." I take a sip of water. "What about Woods?"

He shoves half a taco into his mouth and shrugs.

"You said he was your friend. What happened after you went to jail?" I tilt my head. "Wait. Why were you in jail?"

TJ gulps his water and leans back against his chair. "You ever consider going into journalism?"

I snort and a piece of taco shell lodges itself in my throat. TJ smacks me on the back while I sputter and cough.

I spend the remainder of the night listening to stories from TJ's past. It breaks my heart to hear how awful his foster homes were, and to think about how many other kids have to live in the same kinds of situations. I'm especially upset when he tells me he was homeless. I can't fathom something like that. Alone. No family or friends to help you. Nowhere to live. No food to fill your stomach. I try to picture it, but I just can't.

It's after eleven when an idea pops into my brain. "Do you ever volunteer?"

TJ stifles a yawn. "I do."

"Can I come with you the next time you go?"

"You'd do that?"

"Absolutely." I jump to my feet. "Oh my God. We should have a box for donations at the gym! People can donate food, jackets, gloves, and clothes. Do you have paper and a pen? I'll get a list started. We'll need signs and tubs to carry everything in. Maybe we can put an ad in the newspaper. I can make flyers and hang them around my campus. Oh, and we'll need—"

TJ's lips are on mine. I didn't even see him stand. His hands weave through my hair, pulling me closer. It's a soft, sweet kiss, and then it's over.

I want to keep going, but he's my boss at a job I desperately need. I can't keep muddling the boundary lines. Why are we always two seconds away from kissing? There's attraction, sure, but is that all that keeps drawing me to this man? Whenever we touch, all I want is more. But I don't know if I can handle more.

I rest my forehead against his. "It's getting late. I should go."

He cups my face. "Stay with me tonight."

"I don't think that's a good idea."

"I don't want you driving home this late."

"I'm not that far."

"I promise I'll keep my hands to myself. I can sleep on the couch."

"No. You're not sleeping on the couch in your own apartment. I'll go. It's okay."

"Carla." I hear it in the way he says my name. Feel it in the way his hands tighten around my waist. See it in the way his eyes look into mine with nothing but sincerity.

It's a plea.

And I succumb to it.

TJ loans me a gray T-shirt that reaches my knees. One whiff of his scent in the fabric and I've already made up my mind that he'll never get this shirt back. It's a shame, because he probably looks sexy as hell in it.

His warm body slips into bed and I curl around him, resting my cheek against his bare chest. I ask him to tell me a happy memory he has of his mother. He combs his fingers through my hair while he tells me, and I'm lulled to sleep by his smooth voice, in the safety of his arms.

It's the first night I haven't fallen asleep thinking about Joe or the miscarriage.

So much for not muddling the lines.

Chapter Twenty-Six

THE PAST

"PLEASE SIT DOWN AND TRY TO RELAX."

"Relax? You just told me you have cancer and you're going to die—no, you're *choosing* to die. How do you expect me to relax?"

Reggie drags his fingertips across his beard. "I knew you weren't going to take this well."

I stop pacing and whip around to face him. "Is there another way to take this? Any sane person would have the same reaction. You have cancer, but you're not getting chemo. The doctors give you two months tops." I tap my finger against my chin. "Don't think there's a happy reaction to this news."

"Look, TJ. I know you're scared—"

"Scared? Try fucking furious. How could you hide this from me? How could you not tell me? You always talk about staying away from situations that might trigger my old habits. Don't you think death is a major fucking trigger?"

Reggie rubs his temples. "I know this is going to be difficult for you. But I am going to help you through it. You're not going to fall off the wagon. Everything is going to be fine."

"Everything is not going to be fine!" My voice cracks, throat trying to swallow around the boulder inside it. "You saved me. How can you turn your back on me like this? You always preach about fighting. Why aren't you fighting? You're just giving up. Throwing in the towel. That how it is now?"

"The doctors said the chemo would only prolong my life a little further. It wouldn't cure me. And it would make those last few months miserable. I'd be sick and in pain. That's not how I want to go out."

Rage rips a fresh wound in my chest. I'm spiraling down a dark hole. The only person who had my back in this world is leaving me. I'm back to being alone. Back to a life with no purpose. No help. No love.

Reggie stands and steadies me, holding my face in his huge paws. "You're going to be all right. You've been using me as your crutch for some time. I've gotten you this far. The training wheels are off now, and it's up to you to keep pedaling the rest of the way."

A flood blurs my vision. "I don't want to ride without you."

Reggie pulls me against his shoulder, holding the back of my head with his hand. "I'll always be with you, son. Always."

"What if I fuck up and I need you? What happens when you're not here?"

"You're not going to fuck up, you hear me?" His grip on me tightens. "Promise yourself you won't fuck up, and you won't."

"How do you know?" I ask between sobs.

"Because I believe in you. Now it's time you believe in yourself."

Chapter Twenty-Seven

THE PRESENT

arla

"CARLA EVANS, GET YOUR ASS IN THIS APARTMENT AND TELL ME where you were last night!"

I bury my face in my hands as I hit the top step. "Mal, it's early. Can you take it down an octave, or seven?"

"I most certainly will not. You spent the night with someone and I need to know all the details."

"Coffee first. Talkie later."

She thrusts a steaming mug into my hands and guides me to the couch. "You are not leaving for class until you tell me everything."

I gulp down half my coffee. "Before I say anything, you have to promise to remain calm."

"I promise." She makes an X over her heart.

"Okay." I take a deep breath. "I spent the night at TJ's."

I'm stunned by a sound that I'm sure can only be used by bats to communicate with one another.

"You promised to stay calm. I think you just achieved a higher octave than Mariah Carey."

"I wouldn't have promised that if I'd have known what you were going to say! I knew you were into him. I knew you guys were hiding something."

"We're not hiding anything. We were hanging out and it got late. He didn't want me driving home so I stayed the night. No big deal."

Mal's face contorts. "You had an adult sleepover with the hottest man on earth and all you did was sleep?"

"Yes. Now can I please get ready for class?"

Her head shakes. "I've never been so disappointed in you."

"Good. Considering we just met, I don't want to set the bar too high. Better that you're disappointed now."

She flings a pillow in my direction as I scurry to the bathroom.

I'm not lying to Mallory. All TJ and I did last night was sleep. But my gut tells me it was so much more than that. He opened up to me. He trusted me enough to let me in. And the way he held me while we slept *wasn't* platonic.

I'm entering into uncharted territories. Joe is all I've known. The only one I've ever dated. We were kids when we met. It was innocent and we fell in love. Everything was simple.

This *thing* with TJ isn't comparable. But what is it?

As I step into the shower, I make a mental list of the concrete facts.

I'm attracted to TJ. He's attracted to me. We enjoy spending time in each other's company. That much is clear. Things start getting confusing when I think about the way TJ makes me *feel*.

Joe gave me butterflies, but TJ is a runaway train that's headed straight for me. I don't know if I should jump on or out of the way. I kissed Joe and saw fireworks, but TJ's kiss could burn the whole world to the ground. My relationship with Joe was once comforting and familiar. When I'm around TJ, I don't feel like myself. I can't think straight. It's scary and exhilarating and confusing all at once.

Maybe it's not fair to compare the two. They're vastly different men. Could I see myself with TJ the way I saw my life with Joe? Is that even an option? TJ filled me in on his past, but he never talks about the future. After everything he has been through, is settling down with a wife and a family something he wants?

Questions swarm my mind for the rest of the day. By the time I get to work, it's like an anvil was dropped on my head.

"You okay?" Kimmie asks.

"I just have a headache."

"I have Tylenol if you need it."

"Already exceeded the dosage of ibuprofen for the day."

Her eyebrows lift. "Yikes. So maybe now's not the best time to ask you for advice."

I perk up. "Advice? Of course. What's up?"

"A boy at school asked me to this dance we're having on Halloween."

"And do we like this boy?"

A smile spreads across her face. "We do."

I clap excitedly. "That's great. So what do you need advice about?"

"Everything," she whines. Her head drops to the counter and she buries it with her arms.

"Let's make a list of everything we need to do before Friday." I tear a piece of paper from my notebook. "We'll need to get a costume and shoes. We need nails, hair, and make-up. What else?"

"I need to magically learn how to dance by Friday," she mumbles from her cocoon.

"Girl, don't you worry. Your fairy godmother is at your service."

———

"GIRLS, THIS IS MY FRIEND KIMMIE. KIMMIE, THIS IS CHARLOTTE and Mallory."

Charlotte squeezes Kimmie's shoulder. "We've all been where you are. Don't be nervous. We're going to help you."

Kimmie's shoulders slump. "I feel so pathetic. I don't know how to be girly and pretty like you guys."

"You're already pretty," Mallory says. "And you don't need to be girly. Just be yourself."

I nod. "That's the most important lesson tonight. Don't try to act like someone else. If this boy asked you out, it's because he likes you."

"I think I got your iPod synced," TJ says. He's letting us use the training room in his gym. It has wood floors and wall-to-wall mirrors. It looks like a dance studio. It's perfect.

"You're going to leave now, right?" Kimmie asks.

TJ grins. "You sure you don't want me to stay? I've got some pretty killer dance moves I can teach you." He grabs the back of his neck with one hand, and holds his ankle with his other hand while jerking his knee back and forth.

Kimmie looks horrified. "I never want to see that again."

I laugh and shove TJ toward the door. "Go. You're scaring the poor girl."

"I'm going. I'm going." He winks before closing the door behind him.

Mallory leans in to whisper in my ear. "It's like his wink is directly linked to my vagina. Every time he does it, I feel a zap in my pants."

"TMI, Mal. I don't need to know what happens in your pants."

"Don't act like you're unaffected."

I bite my bottom lip and crouch down by the radio. Oh, I am *so* affected. "Okay, ladies. Let's dance."

I press play on my iPod and the best club songs from the early 2000's blare through the speakers for the next hour. We teach Kimmie some simple steps, like moving from side to side. Then we add in a swaying of the hips. Mallory even shows her what to do when a horny teenage boy tries to bump and grind behind her. We end up doing a lot more laughing than dancing, but that's all Kimmie needs to know: How to have fun and not take this dance too seriously.

"Mal's going to do your make-up," I say. "Charlotte will do your hair, and tomorrow night I'll take you to the mall so we can pick out a dress. Our nail appointments are already set for Friday afternoon."

Kimmie shakes her head with watery eyes. "Thank you, guys. Seriously. I don't know what I'd do without you."

We all hug, and I walk the girls to the exit.

"You coming home tonight, slut?" Mallory asks.

"Yes, I'll be home. I just need to close up here. I'll see you in a little while."

I make sure the front desk is in order and peek inside TJ's office before I leave. "Do you need anything? I'm heading out for the night."

"No, thanks. I'm good." He leans back and rocks in his chair. "Thank you for helping Kimmie. It means the world to her, you know."

"It's no big deal. I don't mind helping."

"It is a big deal. She doesn't have the best support system at home. You're doing more for her than her mother ever did."

"Well, I'm glad I can help."

"You're amazing, Carla."

"You're pretty amazing yourself."

I turn and leave, putting distance between me and the freight train that's barreling straight toward my heart.

Chapter Twenty-Eight

THE PAST

*T*J

"I NEED TO TELL YOU SOME THINGS, SO LET ME GET IT ALL OUT. Don't interrupt me. Got it?"

I keep my eyes trained on the hospital floor and nod. It's hard seeing Reggie like this. Once a strong giant, he's now reduced to a frail man hooked up to machines. It doesn't seem fair.

Life's not fair, Reggie would say. He's accepted his fate. He's at peace with it. I'm not there yet.

"I know you're angry. I know life hasn't been easy for you. But I don't want you to dwell on those things. You didn't deserve any of what happened in your life. You've overcome so much. Focus on that. Focus on what's ahead of you. I know you think you won't be able to continue moving forward without me, but you can and you will. I know it. That's why I'm leaving my gym to you."

My head jerks up. "What?"

"You heard me. Don't fuck this up and let it go to shit just to spite me. I'll haunt your ass. Don't think I won't. Nobody wants a scary black man jumping out at them in the middle of the night."

He rasps out a laugh, but I can't find the humor in this.

"You've shadowed me for long enough. You know how to run things. My clients are now your clients. Help them. They need you. And you need them. You can learn a lot from helping others.

"I'm also leaving you some money. My lawyer will be in contact with you. Buy yourself a house. Meet a girl. Make a family. You can have it all. Don't be afraid to go for it."

Tears well in both our eyes, but I fight to hold mine back.

"You gave me a second chance at being a father. Thank you for that. I couldn't be prouder of your recovery. The fight you have inside you is your best asset. You've fought against the odds. You can achieve anything as long as you tell yourself you can. Believe it, TJ. Believe in yourself."

Reggie reaches for my hand, and when I cover his with mine, my tears make their descent down my face.

"I'll be looking down on you, so make me proud. You hear me?"

I swallow past the lump lodged in my throat and say, "Yes."

"I love you, son. Don't you ever forget that."

"I love you too, Reg. Thank you for saving me."

"Ah, I just helped you. You saved yourself."

I hold his hand as he closes his eyes, and I watch his chest rise and fall for the last time.

———

"Got any other tattoos?"

I shake my head. "Nope. This is my first."

"Mind if I ask what it means?"

"Just lost my good friend. He's looking down on me now, and I need that reminder."

"I'm sorry, man. That's rough."

I swallow the emotion and change the subject. "I thought this would hurt more."

John chuckles. He wipes my shoulder and the needle returns to my skin. "The shoulder is an easy spot. Collar bone and ribcage are pretty painful."

"I kinda like the pain."

"Some of us do."

"This is the first time I've had a needle pierce my skin for a good reason."

"Heroin?"

I nod.

"I was addicted to painkillers for three years. Addiction's a bitch."

"This might be my new addiction."

"It's not a bad one to have, my man. But you'll eventually run out of skin. Then what?"

"Guess I'll have to leave some space open for emergencies."

When John's done, I admire the finished product in the mirror. Reggie's face surrounded by clouds on my shoulder, casting rays of sunlight down my arm.

It's the first of many, and I make my next appointment before I leave.

I miss you, Reggie. And I'm going to make you proud.

Chapter Twenty-Nine

THE PRESENT

arla

"I'M STARTING TO GET NERVOUS."

I glance at the time before sending another text to Kimmie. It goes unanswered, like my previous texts and calls.

TJ's pacing his office like a caged animal. "Tell me one more time what she said at the nail salon."

"We got our nails done. I said I had to go back to work for a few hours. I told her to meet me here at five. She said okay. She seemed excited." I swallow past the lump in my throat. "What are you thinking?"

TJ rakes a hand through his hair for the tenth time, pulling at the ends. "You don't want to know what I'm thinking."

I stand from the chair in front of his desk and grip his shoulders. "Stop pacing. Please. I need you to talk to me."

His eyes slam shut, like it pains him to say the words aloud. "I think something's wrong. We should go to her house."

"I have her address on file." I run out of his office and return in seconds with Kimmie's file.

TJ types the address into his phone and grabs my hand.

Without a word, we climb into his truck. TJ follows his GPS and in ten minutes, he pulls off the main road. Gravel crunches under his tires while we search for Kimmie's mobile home.

"There!" I point out my window and fling off my seatbelt.

TJ's hand wraps around my wrist. "Carla, I need you to wait here."

"No way. I'm coming with you."

He pinches the bridge of his nose. "I don't know what we're walking into. I'd rather you stayed in the truck."

"I said I'm coming with you." I yank free from his grasp and hop out of the truck.

TJ beats me to the door and knocks. "Kimmie? Are you in there?"

I cup my hands around my eyes as I squint through the window. "There's a light on, but I can't see anything."

His knocks turn to pounds. "Kimmie! It's TJ. Open up!"

I push past him and try the doorknob. The door swings open, but I remain frozen where I stand. Closing my eyes, I inhale a shaky breath.

"I'll go in first," TJ says.

The lights are on in the kitchen, but nobody's there. Two bowls with milk sit on the kitchen table beside an opened box of cereal.

I follow TJ into the narrow hallway. There's not much space, and he looks like a giant.

"Kimmie?" I call. "Are you here? We have to get you ready for the dance tonight." My hands are shaking. The deafening sound of blood pounding in my ears fills the eerie silence.

The bathroom door is open, but empty.

TJ points to the bedrooms. "Let's check this one first. Stay behind me."

I nod, hoping my face looks braver than I feel. Holding my breath, I count to three while TJ's turns the knob.

One.

Two.

Three.

It's dark inside. I feel around for the light switch, but when it flips on, it reveals nothing. One room left.

TJ opens the door and light spills out into the hallway. He's blocking my view, unmoving, hand still holding onto the doorknob. Several seconds tick by before he rushes into the room.

I watch as he drops to the floor.

I watch as he checks for a pulse.

I watch as he stands and stalks over to the dresser.

It's like there's a delay between what I'm seeing and what's actually happening. There must be, because I'm unable to react. Unable to move. Unable to process what I'm witnessing.

The crash of the dresser flipping over snaps me out of my freeze frame. Drawers open, clothes spilling out onto the floor. TJ drops back down and cradles Kimmie in his arms, rocking her back and forth.

A pile of what looks like lumpy oatmeal sits on the carpet beside them. A needle gleams in the light.

It all hits me at once. My hands cover my mouth as my knees buckle.

"Call 911." TJ's voice is low.

"Is she ... is ..." The words are caught in my throat. I don't want to ask.

Tears stream down TJ's cheeks as he presses his lips to the top of Kimmie's head. "She's gone."

"No. She can't ... she can't be. We have to get ready for the dance."

TJ's eyes meet mine, apologetic and filled with sorrow. "She's gone, Carla. We're too late."

I reach for Kimmie's arm and press two fingers to her wrist. Squeezing my eyes shut, I wait for a pulse. I wait and I wait, willing the feeling of even the faintest twitch. But nothing comes. Her skin already feels cool to the touch.

"No," I say between sobs. "No."

TJ lays her body gently on the carpet and caresses her hair. Then his arms are around me.

"No." It's the only word I can muster. How can this be? How can Kimmie be dead? I just saw her at the nail salon. She was fine. Everything was fine. How did this happen?

I bury my face in TJ's chest, hot tears soaking his shirt.

"I need to call the police. Do you want to wait in the truck?"

I shake my head. "How ... what happened?"

TJ sucks in a staggered breath and slips his phone out of his pocket. "Sometimes, when you use heroin, it makes you sick. It looks like she passed out on her back, threw up, and ... she choked." His gaze drops to his phone as he dials.

I crawl to Kimmie and hold her head in my lap. Moisture wells in my eyes and the tears roll off my cheeks, dripping into her golden hair. I glance at her perfectly manicured nails and choke back a sob. She was supposed to be dancing tonight. Laughing. Having fun. She's just a kid. Had her whole life in front of her. How can her life be over?

My phone buzzes in my back pocket, but I don't have the courage to answer it. I know it's Mallory checking in. How am I going to break this news to her and Charlotte? They're going to be devastated.

I'm devastated.

My watery eyes drift to TJ. He's devastated too.

His head hangs, staring at the phone long after he ended the call. His heart is breaking. I can see it all over his face. Feel it rolling off him in waves of grief. He feels responsible.

I know this because I feel the same.

———

It's late when we pull in front of the gym.

TJ and I haven't spoken a word since we left Kimmie's house. The only time he let go of my hand was when we climbed into his truck. He held my hand when the police arrived. He held my hand as the coroner zippered Kimmie into the black bag. He held my hand as he drove. He held my hand while I called Mallory. It's almost as if he's afraid I'll float away, like a balloon on a string when you release it.

Or maybe he's the balloon. Holding onto me grounds him, keeps him from disappearing into the atmosphere. Either way, I'm gripping his hand just as tight.

He doesn't ask me to stay the night. He doesn't have to. I won't leave him alone tonight.

We enter the gym and shuffle up the stairs into his apartment. Stripping off our clothes in silence, we lay on the bed facing each other. My lids are heavy and swollen, yet the tears continue to fall. TJ strokes my cheek with his thumb, gazing through my eyes and penetrating my soul.

Sometime after midnight, I ask, "Is this my fault?"

"No, Carla. How could you ever think that?"

"I was the last one to see her. I didn't notice anything wrong. I should've seen it. I should've been there for her."

TJ draws me closer, stroking my face, my hair. "You need to understand that this had nothing to do with you. This did not happen because of anything you did or didn't do. Kimmie was an addict, and sometimes this is what happens to addicts."

"Could this happen to you?"

"It won't."

My lower lip trembles. The more I try to imagine my life without TJ in it, the more impossible it becomes. "I don't want this to happen to you."

TJ opens his mouth to speak but I cut him off. "No. Please. Promise me you'll tell me if you need help. Promise me I won't ever find you like ... like that. Please."

"Shhh. It's okay." TJ envelops me in his arms, pressing my cheek against his bare chest. "That won't ever be me. Don't worry your pretty head about that."

"I need you to promise me." I lift my chin to look into his eyes. "Promise me you'll talk to me if you need help."

"I promise." His nose nuzzles the tip of mine. "Even though I don't deserve your help."

"You deserve everything good in this world."

TJ's cradles my face and presses his soft, plump lips to mine.

We fall asleep soon after.

"CLOSE YOUR EYES. TAKE A FEW SLOW, DEEP BREATHS. RELAX YOUR mind and listen to my voice."

I'd laugh if I wasn't so nervous. Here I am, on my therapist's couch, about to do some hypnosis voodoo shit. All that's missing is the swinging pocket watch. *Look into my eyes.* Great. Now I'm envisioning Dracula when I'm supposed to be relaxing my mind.

But how am I supposed to relax when I'm about to recount what happened the day my mom died? That's a memory I've stuffed down so far, I don't even know where to begin.

But I promised Reggie I'd make him proud. I held his hand on his death bed and promised him I'd keep fighting. If this is what I need to do, consider it done.

And so I begin. "On my thirteenth birthday, we were about to have cake. Mom, Dad, and me. My birthday was never a big deal growing up. Mom tried to make it special. Balloons, cake, a present to open after dinner. But Dad always found a way to ruin it.

"That particular day, Dad started complaining because he hated ice cream cake. Mom told him it was my favorite. Vanilla and chocolate with the crunchies in the middle." I smile but it fades just as quickly. "Dad slapped her for talking back to him. He said it didn't matter what my favorite kind of cake was, because he was the one who paid for it. He always threw it in her face, the fact that she didn't work, though he'd never let her get a job.

"It made me so mad to see him hurt her, especially over something as irrelevant as cake. Sometimes, she knew when to keep quiet. He'd hit her once, and it would end there. But that night, she wanted to defend me. She told him he didn't have to eat the cake if he didn't like it. That's when the night took a turn.

"It's all a blur now. His glass of scotch smashing against the wall. Mom screaming at me to go to my room. I tried to stop him. I jumped on his back but that seemed to make him even angrier. Then he took her by the throat. I pulled on his arm, but he shoved me so hard I lost my balance and hit my head on the side table."

My body tenses, hands ball into fists.

"It's okay, TJ. I'm here. You're safe. Tell me what happens next."

I suck in a breath, and force myself to go back to that moment. That horrific memory. The event that changed my life forever ...

MY EYELIDS FLUTTER OPEN. I BLINK UNTIL THE WHITE POPCORN CEILING comes into focus.

I lift my hand to the source of the throbbing pain on the side of my head. Deep red blood glistens on my fingertips. My eyes avert to the end table beside the couch and there's blood smeared along one of the sharp corners. I roll over to check if there's any blood on the carpet. The Monster will be mad if I ruin his carpet.

I try to sit up, but a sound immobilizes me. It's the only thing I can hear over the ringing in my ears from the splitting headache I now have.

Gagging.

Gagging is different from gasping. I'd gasped for air after The Monster held my head under water last month. Gasping means you're getting oxygen into your lungs.

This isn't that.

Mom isn't getting any oxygen. She's losing it.

I want to stand but my legs won't work. My brain wants to take action but my body is paralyzed. I'm used to this. I've lived in fear my entire life. Fear traps you inside your own body, holding you prisoner, convincing you of lies that sound like the truth. Fear controls me. I let it, because I don't know what else I can do.

I remain on the floor as my gaze travels upward, afraid to look, yet afraid to miss it. The Monster's back is to me. He's in the same position I left him in when he shoved me to the ground. I'd tried to stop him. I'd tried like hell. But what match is a scrawny thirteen-year old for such evil?

With his vice grip around Mom's neck, her toes dangle a few inches above the tile. Her arms hang limp at her sides.

She should use her feet to kick him. She should try to break his grip around her throat.

But she's not fighting. Not even in this extreme of a moment. She's not fighting for herself. She's not fighting for me.

That's what fear does. It overpowers your fight.

Mom's eyes lock with mine now. I expect her to convey some telepathic message asking me for help. But I can tell from the look in her eyes she doesn't want help. She has already given up. The only thing her eyes say to me is I'm sorry.

I'm sorry, too, Mom. I'm sorry you married The Monster. I'm sorry you weren't strong enough to fight him. I'm sorry you never took us away from him. I'm sorry I have to watch you die at the hand of the person who took a vow to love and to cherish you for all the days of your lives.

Most of all, I'm sorry I'm so helpless.

An eerie silence descends upon the room. Tears stream from her bulging, bloodshot eyes as her face turns another shade of purple. Mom is drifting away, and I'm glad. I'm glad she doesn't have to endure another second of torture. I'm not surprised by my relief. Mom didn't deserve this life. Now she'll float up to heaven, the only place worthy of a woman like her.

I love you, Mom.

Reality sets in. Once The Monster is done with her, he'll come for me. Adrenaline flows through my veins as fear releases me. I army-crawl to the end table for the phone. My shaky, blood-stained fingers press the three numbers I'm used to dialing. We should've had the police on speed dial. I slide the phone under the couch so The Monster won't hear the person answer on the other end of the line. I don't have to say anything. They'll come soon. They always come.

A loud, hollow crack sounds throughout the room. I know what it is before I even look. I've heard Mom's skull crack against the tile floor enough times to recognize the sound. Mom's lifeless body lay at The Monster's feet in a heap. Long, brown waves frame her heart-shaped face. With her delicate features and cascading hair, I used to tell her she was as beautiful as an angel. Now, she looks like an angel of death. Her skin has a grayish-blue tint to it, except for the red streaks around her neck where The Monster's fingers left their marks. His parting gift, so she can take him with her.

A puddle seeps out from underneath her body, no longer in control of her bowels. Bruises line her arms, some a deep purple and some a yellowish green, telling stories new and old about the pain she has endured at the hands of a monster. Our monster.

Mom's eyes are open. I want to crawl over to her and close them. They aren't staring at me anymore. They aren't staring at anything. The soul behind them has been set free.

The Monster's rage subsides like a change in tide, replaced by the numbness of the alcohol. He slides down the wall and sits beside Mom's body. He's too much of a coward to look at her. I want to hold her hand. I want to lay with her. But I don't. Fear tells me to stay where I am so The Monster isn't reminded that I'm still here. Fear prevents me from having my final moment with my mother, though it's keeping me safe. I hug my knees to my chest as my silent tears fall. I don't want The Monster to see me cry. He hates it when I cry.

Red and blue flashing lights illuminate the room.

I take pleasure in watching an officer handcuff him, committing the image to memory. Justice is finally being served, after all these years. A sense of calm washes over me.

It's over.

The Monster is gone.

But so is my mother.

I crawl to her. Brushing her hair away from her face, I press my lips to her forehead. Her skin isn't cold, yet it doesn't feel like her. Her usual warm, vanilla scent is gone.

She is gone.

Sour sickness churns in the pit of my stomach. I scramble to the bathroom down the hall and heave into the toilet. I stare at the chunks of vomit floating in the water, remembering how Mom used to rub my back in soothing circles whenever I got sick.

No one is here to rub my back now.

No one is here to comfort me.

I am alone.

I flush the toilet and rinse my mouth out in the sink. My reflection stares back at me in the mirror while I steady my breath. Big blue eyes. Dark hair. I look like the younger version of The Monster.

If a monster creates you, are you then part monster?

When I step out of the bathroom, Detective Woods is leaning against the wall waiting for me. I don't make eye contact with him. Instead, I study his shoes. His shoes are always so shiny.

Woods places his large hand on my shoulder. "I'm so sorry about your mom."

I nod.

"Thomas, I need you to come with me. Once the EMT checks you out, of course."

I need to give my statement. I know the routine well. Only this time, I've witnessed a murder.

I follow Woods back into the living room. Yellow numbers now surround Mom's body on the floor. My house no longer looks like my home. It's a crime scene. I suppose it always was.

My eyes settle on the melting ice cream cake on the dining room table. An hour ago, Mom was singing Happy Birthday to me and Dad was explaining how turning thirteen meant I was a man.

Yeah. Today's my birthday.

The flash of a camera interrupts my thoughts. Who would want that job, taking pictures of dead bodies?

Woods puts his arm around my shoulders. "Come on, kid. You don't need to watch this."

It's too late, I want to say. I've already seen too much.

More than anyone should.

Nothing will ever be the same again. Not that I want it to be as it was before. Living with a violent drunk for a father and a weak, abused mother isn't a life I want to go back to ... but where will I go from here? Who will want me now?

A monster's child.
A monster child.

Sobs rack my body. Uncontrollable emotions unleash, flooding every cell in my being. My hands clutch my chest, as if I can physically stop everything from pouring out.

I'm hemorrhaging.

A release of all the bad.

Pain.

Fear.

Rage.

Guilt.

"You're all right, TJ," my therapist says. "You're in my office. You're safe. You're going to be okay."

How? I wonder.

How will I ever be okay?

Chapter Thirty-One

THE PRESENT

arla

"HAVE YOU SEEN TJ AT ALL THIS WEEK?"

I shake my head and cast a longing look in the direction of the room TJ's locked inside.

It's the room we taught Kimmie how to dance in just last week. Sadness pricks my heart. "He's been in there."

Tanner's eyebrows collapse. "Any clue what he's doing inside?"

"No. He comes out to train a client, and then he goes right back in."

He glances at the watch on his wrist. "All right. Keep me posted. I'm worried about him."

I nod. "Me too."

Tanner gestures to the overflowing box by the door on his way out. "Great idea with the donation box, by the way."

I muster a smile and say, "Thanks. Tell Charlotte I'll call her later."

It's been a tough week. We said goodbye to a sweet, innocent girl as she was lowered into the ground. To say TJ's taking Kimmie's death poorly would be an understatement. He has been keeping to himself, more than usual. *Working on a project* was all he'd said to me.

I don't know much about how an addict falls off the wagon, but I'm worried about him.

At the end of every shift, I tap my knuckles against the locked door. I call for him and wait. Then I head home.

Tonight is no different. After knocking and staring at the closed door for several minutes, I walk back to the front desk and collect my things. I'm about to leave when the door cracks open. TJ slips through and closes it behind him.

He doesn't notice me until he gets closer. He stops mid-stride, head down, attention trained on the ground.

"Hey." I survey his appearance. Wrinkled shirt, shorts smudged with paint, baseball cap pulled low over his eyes.

"Thought you left."

"Just about to. Need any help in there?" I twist a strand of hair around my finger. "Maybe some company?"

"Thanks, but I'm all finished for the night."

"Want to grab dinner? I'm itching for a slice of pizza."

"Not tonight."

"Come on. You need to eat." I nudge him with my elbow, a feeble attempt at playfulness. "Gotta keep feeding those muscles."

"Not tonight."

He shuffles past me and that's when I notice. A gasp leaves my lips as I grip onto his forearm. "Oh my God. TJ, your face."

He pulls his hat down further, turning his face away. "It's nothing."

I stretch onto my toes to get a better look, clutching his face in my hands. His left eyelid, almost completely swollen shut, is a deep purple. There's more bruising along his jaw and a gash on his top lip.

"What happened to you? Who did this?"

"Don't worry about it." He backs away and my hands fall to my sides.

"I do worry. I'm worried about you."

"Why, because I'm an addict? You assume I'll resort to using just because someone died?"

His harsh tone stuns me. "No. I'm sorry. That's not ... that's not what I meant. I just—"

"Save it." His office door slams shut, the click of the lock like a shot to my sternum.

————

AS IF THE ROLLERCOASTER OF EMOTIONS I'M ON THIS WEEK ISN'T enough, Joe's texts come in more frequently.

JOE: PLEASE ANSWER ME.
   Joe: How's New York?
   Joe: When are you coming back?
   Joe: I miss you.
   Joe: Do you miss me?
   Joe: I ended things with Brianna.
   Joe: Let's talk. Don't throw everything away.

I TOSS MY PHONE ONTO THE COUCH CUSHION BESIDE ME. "THAT LAST one kills me. As if I'm the one who walked away from what we had. Does he actually believe that? Or is he trying to get a reaction out of me?"

"You should block his ass," Mallory says.

"Or talk to him," Charlotte chimes in. "Closure will help you move on."

"The idea of rehashing everything he put me through ..." I shake my head. "I don't think I can do that."

"Plus, he'll just feed you more excuses." Mallory rolls her eyes as she crams a handful of Doritos into her mouth. "He doesn't deserve to explain himself."

I can tell Charlotte disagrees. She always looks down at her lap and tucks her hair behind her ear when she stops herself from saying what she's thinking.

I sigh, flopping back onto the couch. "Honestly, I don't even care about Joe right now. I'm too worried about TJ to think about much else."

"He's still not talking to you?" Mallory asks.

"No, but trust me—the slamming door speaks volumes."

"He's just going through a hard time," Charlotte says. "He knew Kimmie for a while. He was her sponsor. That's gotta feel awful."

"I know. I just wish he'd let me in. Help him."

Mallory stands, brushing orange crumbs onto the rug. She pauses and looks at me. "I'll vacuum later, I swear."

I laugh and shake my head, knowing I'll get to it before she does.

"Why don't we stop sitting around and wasting time talking about stupid boys? Let's go do something."

Charlotte holds her hand up. "I don't want to go to a bar."

"So we won't. Let's do something different."

Plan B pops into my mind and a light flicks on. TJ took me sky diving. If it weren't for him, I probably wouldn't have gone through with it. Why am I sitting around waiting for someone to help me complete my list? I don't need help living my life. This is my life. And I'm wasting it on this couch.

All a girl really needs are her friends, and I've got 'em right here.

"Let's get tattoos."

Mallory's screech sounds through the apartment. "Yes! That's the kind of shit I'm talking about, roomie! Let's do it!"

"Since when do you want to get a tattoo?" Charlotte asks.

I hike a shoulder. "Since now. I'm trying to live in the moment, remember?"

A frown tugs at her lips. "Can't we live in the moment without needles burning into our skin? We can watch a movie."

Mallory yanks Charlotte's arm until she's standing. "You can watch us live in the moment. It'll be just like you're watching a movie."

She sighs. "Tanner got his tattoo done by TJ's friend. At least go to someone who we know is good."

I stand and nod, excitement surging through me. "Let's do this."

The excitement soon wears off and is replaced by nerves once we're in Mallory's car.

Why did I suggest this? What was I thinking?

More importantly, how bad is this going to hurt?

Charlotte swivels in the passenger seat to face me. "Your mom is going to kill you, you know."

"You're like the fish from *The Cat in the Hat*," Mallory says.

Charlotte shoots her a glare, which only looks adorable on her sweet face. "And that's a bad thing? He knew it was wrong for those kids to let a giant cat stranger into the house."

"Come on, Char," Mallory whines. "Don't suck the fun out of this. People get tattoos all the time. Plus, this is way better than staying home and listening to that one cry about her boy problems."

I make eye-contact with her in the rear-view mirror. "Hey!"

Her eyes roll before flicking back to the road. *"Wahh, my hot ex won't stop texting me. Wahh, my boss is ridiculously sexy."*

"Okay, first of all—I don't sound like that. Secondly ... well ... I don't have a second thing, but the first one still stands."

"I'm just saying ... you've got two dudes vying for your attention. Share the wealth, homie."

"You want Joe? Be my guest."

Charlotte and Mallory exchange glances.

"What?"

"Oh, nothing. It's just funny how you offered Joe over TJ." Charlotte throws a wink over her shoulder.

"I was just trying to make a point. Joe isn't some amazing guy trying to woo me. He's a jerk who left me high and dry."

"And TJ?" Mallory asks. "What's he?"

I gaze out the window as we come to a stop in front of the tattoo shop. "Good question," I mutter.

"What was that? Couldn't hear you."

"I said he's my boss. Now let's go before I change my mind."

Chapter Thirty-Two

THE PAST

"Do you love her?" my therapist asks.

I shrug. "I don't know. Never been in love before."

"But you have feelings for her."

"I do."

Merritt Adams is the first woman I've ever developed feelings for. Twenty-five years of my life and she's the first one. I knew it from the first moment she walked into my gym.

Tanner brought her to me. Said she was drinking a lot and couldn't stop. After everything she'd been through, I couldn't blame the girl for wanting to numb the pain. Her mother abandoned her when Merritt was thirteen. When she turned twenty, her father committed suicide. Slit his wrists in the bathtub. That's how she found him.

For two months, I've trained her.

And for two months, I've wanted to make her mine.

"Has she given you the impression that she has feelings for you?"

I shake my head. "But she broke up with her boyfriend."

"The one in California?"

"That would be the one." The selfish man that stayed in California to pursue his dream of becoming a rock star, while his girlfriend got drunk every night to try to escape her demons. The same selfish man who let her leave California, alone, at her lowest point, so he could continue living the high life without her.

"What are your thoughts on that?"

He's a stupid fucking idiot. "Don't have many thoughts about their relationship. But I want to talk to her now that it's over. Tell her how I feel."

"Do you think a former addict like yourself should be with someone who's still recovering from her own addiction?"

I shrug. "You're the shrink. I don't know what the fuck I'm doing. That's why I'm here. I need your advice."

He chuckles and slips off his glasses. "You know I can't tell you what to do, TJ. I offer counseling. Make you ask yourself important questions, see things from different perspectives."

"But if I want your professional opinion on the matter?"

"Ms. Adams is an alcoholic. I understand why you're drawn to her. You've both experienced the loss of a parent. You've both been deeply hurt by the other parent. You see a lot of yourself in her. You share a connection that goes deeper than most. But I'd be worried about your stability if you entered into a relationship with her."

"And why is that?" I ask.

"I've known you for several years now. I've learned many things about you. But one thing that sticks out the most is your passion for helping people. You're a fixer. This stems from the guilt you harbor for not being able to save your mother. Naturally, you're going to be attracted to people who need help. Damsels in distress, if you will.

"But just because you're attracted to someone doesn't necessarily mean you should be with her. It doesn't mean she's right for you. The person you should be looking for is someone who doesn't need your help. Someone who stands strong on her own, and who pushes you to be a better version of yourself."

I laugh. "Not sure that's in the cards for me, doc."

"It might not be. But you owe it to yourself to try."

———

TONIGHT'S A BIG NIGHT.

Merritt recently reconnected with her mother after almost eight years. The first time they talked, Merritt fell off the wagon—got wasted alone in her apartment. Tonight, they're attempting to talk again. And I'm going to be here to make sure nothing bad happens.

I'm also going to tell Merritt how I feel about her.

My therapist doesn't think it's a smart idea. To be honest, I'm not sure it is either. But I feel something I've never felt before, and I'd be a fool not to try and see where it could go.

I'm sitting on the steps that lead to Merritt's apartment, waiting for her mother to leave. I don't hear any screaming, so I take that as a good sign. An hour passes, and I don't mind. It gives me time to think about what I want to say.

The door cracks open and her mother steps outside. She pauses when she sees me, probably wondering who the scary man with all the tattoos is. I stand and step aside to let her pass.

Merritt's head peers out of the doorway, her face twisting in confusion. "How long have you been sitting out here?"

I shrug and shove my shaking hands into my pockets. "It's a nice night. I wasn't keeping track of the time."

She joins me in the brisk air and sits on the top landing, patting the space beside her.

"How did it go?"

"It actually went really well." Merritt recounts their conversation, and I'm overcome with pride. Instead of slipping into old habits, she sounds stronger. Happier. I can't help but feel like I had something to do with it. Who knows where she'd be if Tanner hadn't come to me for help.

Merritt rests her elbows on her knees, propping her head up with her hands. "My mother made me think twice about breaking up with Chase. Now I'm left with this feeling like I don't know if I made the right choice or not."

My heart drops down the flight of stairs below. I watch as it tumbles, cracking a little more with each concrete step it hits.

I can't tell her how I feel. Not if she's still in love with her ex.

So I do the right thing and say, "To me, the choice is crystal clear. You have to ask yourself one question: Do you love him?"

"Of course I do."

My chest clenches, nothing but a gaping hole now. "Then you need to fight for what you love. You're a warrior, remember?"

A smile spreads across her face. The smile that makes my stomach ache whenever I look at her. "Thanks for coming to check on me," she says.

"Any time, doll face."

"You wouldn't be here if you had a life, you know." She leans in and nudges me with her shoulder, forever teasing me about not having a life outside of work.

"If it weren't for Chase, you *would* be my life." There. I said it. Now she knows. She knows how I feel and she can decide where to go from here.

Her jaw ticks open before she catches it and clamps it shut. Her big brown eyes are wide, locked on mine.

Normally, I tell people to fight for what they want. But judging by the look on her face, she doesn't feel the same about me. She loves *him*. The only time you can't fight for what you love is when she's in love with someone else.

"I didn't know," she says.

"I didn't want you to know."

"I'm so sorry. I can't—"

"I know." I cut her off because I know what she's going to say, and it will only hurt more to hear her say it. "I know."

"You have done so much for me, TJ. I don't know how I can ever repay you."

I stand and stretch, attempting to seem nonchalant about this whole thing. "You can repay me by staying sober. Stop running away from your feelings. Your avoidance is your downfall."

She nods, rising with me. "So, we're cool? I'll see you tomorrow at the gym?"

"You will." I wink and trot down the stairs, collecting the pieces of my heart as I go.

Maybe love isn't meant for me. After everything I've been through, how could I think otherwise?

I'm still a statistic, after all.

Chapter Thirty-Three

THE PRESENT

arla

"You did what?"

I hold the phone away from my ear until the shrill sound of my mother's voice stops. "I got a tattoo. It's not that big a deal."

"Carla, are you on drugs?"

I choke out a laugh. "What? Why would I be on drugs?"

"You're not acting like yourself. They say the first sign of drug use is erratic behavior."

"Who is *they*?"

"Don't get snarky with me, young lady. Tell me the truth. What is going on with you?"

I blow a puff of air through my lips. "Mom, I swear I'm not on drugs. I just ... I guess I'm trying to find myself, if that makes sense. I was with Joe for so long. I need to figure out how my life is going to be without him in it."

"And how is your life going without him? Are you happy?"

I slump onto the counter, fingers making small circles on my temple. "I can't gauge my happiness right now. But I can tell you that

I'm doing okay. I'm working, going to school, and hanging out with my friends. Everything's good here."

"Good, baby. That's all I can ask, I suppose. I know heartbreak is tough but you're strong. You'll get through it. You'll see."

I smile. "I know I will. I miss you, Mom."

"I miss you too. We should start booking your trip home for the holidays."

"I'm clocking out of work right now. We'll talk about it soon."

"All right. Love you, baby."

"Love you."

I end the call and toss my phone into my purse. When I step outside, Tanner's Mustang roars into the parking lot.

I walk to the driver's side and say, "If you're looking for TJ, I haven't seen him all day."

He winces as he jerks his thumb toward the back seat. "I have him."

I peer into the back of Tanner's car and gasp at the heap of muscles and tattoos laid out across the back seat. "What happened?"

Tanner swings the door open and steps outside. "TJ called me and said he needed a ride. The address he gave me wasn't in the best neighborhood. Two dudes carried him out looking like this."

"What did they say?"

Tanner exhales and runs a hand through his hair. "He got jumped after a fight. Three against one."

"Why the hell are you here? He needs a hospital."

Tanner shakes his head. "TJ said he'd get into trouble if he goes to the hospital. He begged me not to. Said he didn't want anyone to find out about this."

"Let's get him out. He might need stitches or have a concussion." *Or worse.*

Tanner pushes his seat forward and pulls TJ out by his legs. The sounds of TJ's agonizing groans claw at my chest. When Tanner slings TJ's lifeless arm around his neck and hoists him out of the car, my stomach rolls and I cover my mouth with both hands.

Oh my God.

His face. The blood. So much blood. There isn't enough light out here to tell where the source of it is. His clothes are torn and blood-stained. He looks like he was dragged down a gravel road from the back of a truck.

"Get the door."

I tear my eyes from TJ's red-streaked face and sprint to the door. Tanner carries him up the stairs to his apartment while I grab the first-aid kit from his office.

Tanner's propping him up against the sink in the bathroom when I return. "Can you stand, buddy?"

TJ groans. "I'm fine." He sways but remains upright without Tanner's help. "Need to sleep this off."

Illuminated under the bathroom bulbs, TJ's face glistens like red stained glass. The eye that was swollen shut the other day looks even worse, puffier, with fresh bruises. The other eye is covered in blood from a cut above his brow. The gash on his top lip reopened, lip swollen to double its size.

My heart thrashes wildly against my chest. TJ's hurt, and it goes so much deeper than what I can see. His terrorizing mental pain caused him to seek out physical pain. Sure, he got jumped, but I know part of him welcomes this—thinks he deserves it.

Will I ever be able to show him that he doesn't?

"The last thing you need to do is sleep," I say.

TJ lifts his chin, eyelids straining to peel open at the sound of my voice. "Carla." He reaches a dirty hand out, brushing his fingertips against my cheek. "My Carla."

Goosebumps break out across my skin, heat sizzling wherever he touches. Even beaten to a bloody pulp, the man is the sexiest thing I've ever seen.

I look up to meet Tanner's questioning gaze. "I can get him cleaned up. I'll stay with him tonight. But he might need to go to the hospital."

"No hospital," TJ murmurs, still caressing my face. "Just you."

"Are you sure you can take care of him?" Tanner asks. "I can stay if you need me to help."

"I've got this."

Tanner nods. "Keep me updated."

"I will."

After a deep breath, I open the first-aid kit and line up everything I'll need on the counter.

"You're not going to put peroxide on me, are you?"

I arch an eyebrow. "The big, tough fighter is afraid of a little burning?"

TJ chuckles but then winces, clutching his ribs.

Sobering immediately, I gather the hem of his shirt in my hands and lift. Another gasp leaves me when I'm hit with the sight of the deep-purple marks along his ribcage. Tiny rocks stick to parts of his skin atop red scrapes.

The image of TJ on the ground assaults my mind. Curled up in a ball, taking hit after hit, kick after kick, alone and helpless. It's almost too much to bear. Shaking it from my thoughts, I try to keep my focus on the task before me.

"Let's get you in the shower." The water will wash away the blood smears and dirt, and I'll be able to assess the severity of his wounds. I tug TJ's shirt over his head, careful not to rub the cotton against his face, and lean into the tub to turn the water on.

When I turn back around, TJ's struggling to push his shorts down, barely able to bend at the waist. I help them down the rest of the way, sucking in a breath as I peel off his boxers. *Now's not the time for sexy thoughts, Carla.* Especially not when TJ's gazing down at me, wearing a smirk on his bruised lips.

Once he's undressed, I wrap my arm around his waist and help him under the hot stream. I'm fully dressed but I don't stop to think about it. I lather a washcloth with soap and rub it in soft circles around TJ's shoulders and back.

"Turn around," I say, and scrub the blood and dirt from his chest.

"Too good, Carla. You're too good." TJ mumbles the entire time I clean him, each word penetrating my heart like an arrow. His fingers brush the wet hair out of my eyes, and sweep down to my lips. "I want you so bad."

I lift onto my toes, letting him occupy himself with touching my face, knowing this next part is going to hurt. I dab the washcloth around the cut on his forehead, cringing when he grunts and grinds his teeth together.

I go as fast and as gingerly as I can, making note of the areas I'll need to bandage once he's dry. "Almost done."

"Never want you to be done. I want to keep you forever."

"They knocked your head pretty good, didn't they?" I refuse to give in to the things he's saying, no matter how badly I want to eat up every last word. Not now. Not yet.

I squirt shampoo into my hands and massage his scalp with my fingertips. His eyes close and he lets out a low groan. Tipping his head back, I rinse the suds from his hair.

One of his hands snakes around my waist while the other is splayed on the tile to hold himself up. He crushes me against his body, gaze heated and locked on mine. Steam and water and desire fill the space around us.

"TJ—"

"I don't deserve you."

A heavy sigh pushes from my mouth. "Come on. Let's get you dried off."

With a towel around his waist, I bandage the gash on his head and treat the scrapes on his ribs. His lip stopped bleeding, so I dab ointment on it and call it good. I help him step into his boxers next. When I'm all finished, he's sitting up in bed holding an ice pack on his eye with another strapped around his torso.

"I really wish you'd let me take you to the hospital for an x-ray. Your ribs might be broken. You could have internal bleeding."

"I'm fine," he says.

"You're not fine. Nothing about this is fine."

"Stop pacing. You're making me dizzy."

I cross my arms over my chest. "Oh, it's my pacing that's making you dizzy? You sure it's not the concussion?"

A smirk forms on his lips, and it only infuriates me more. "So angry." He pats the mattress beside him. "Lay with me."

I keep my scowl in place, grateful that he can't see my heart stretching toward him. "I need to clean up the bathroom and get out of these wet clothes."

He pats the bed again. "Leave it. I need you."

Looking at him lying there, so battered and broken, my resolve melts away. "Fine. Google said it's safe to sleep after a concussion as long as you're able to talk and your pupils aren't dilated."

"Told you I'm fine."

"Yeah, well, it also said you could be dead by morning if you're bleeding internally. So, hopefully I'll see you when the sun comes up." I yank one of his T-shirts over my head and slip into bed beside him.

He chuckles and then winces as I turn out the light.

———

THE NEXT MORNING, I'M WOKEN BY THE SCENT OF BACON WAFTING through TJ's bedroom door. I sit up in his empty bed, digging the heel of my palm into my eye.

I don't know what time it was when I finally let myself fall asleep last night. I'd stayed up, fighting my drooping eyelids, listening to TJ's breaths while he slept.

I slink down the hallway and into the kitchen. *Good Lord.* TJ's standing in front of the stove in nothing but his white boxer briefs. His hair is a disheveled mess. Blood is seeping through the gauze on his ribs. I rub my chest, the dull ache where my heart pounds at the mere sight of him.

As if he can feel the weight of my gaze, he turns around and slays me with a smile. His poor face is a torn-up mess, but his dimples break through. "Morning, gorgeous."

I thrust a hand through the tangled mop on my head. His eyes flick to the hem of his shirt that's riding up over my panties, and I fight to ignore the rush of blood that creeps into my cheeks.

"You should be in bed," I say taking a seat at the table.

"Says the woman who stayed up to watch me sleep all night." He deposits a plate in front of me. Pancakes, scrambled eggs, and bacon. He even chopped up strawberries.

My eyebrows lift. "This smells an awful lot like an apology."

"I was going more for the smell of gratitude."

"You don't have to thank me for taking care of you." I stab a pancake with my fork and dig in. I didn't get to eat dinner with everything that happened last night, and I'm starving.

"I do," he says, easing himself into the seat next to me. "You didn't have to stay here and do what you did. Not after the way I've been treating you these past two weeks."

"The least you can do is tell me what happened."

His chest rises and falls, and then his shoulders slump in defeat. "I've been fighting. It's ... something I do. When things get hard."

My brows pinch together. "Fighting, like you're picking fights in bars?"

"Underground fighting. Like I used to."

"The illegal kind?"

"Yes. Last night, I won the fight. Made a couple hundred bucks. Then the loser and his friends jumped me on the way out. Stole the money."

"Why are you doing this? It's not like you need the money."

"Sometimes, I get a craving. When I lose someone I care about, I want to shoot up or have a drink. It's my trigger. At least that's what my therapist calls it." He breaks eye-contact, chin dropping so he doesn't have to look at me. "I'm fucked up, Carla. I'll always be fucked up. There's nothing you can do to change that."

"Who said anything about changing it?"

"I know you want to help me. Fix me. But you can't."

I drop my fork onto the table and level him with a look. "I'm here because you're hurt and I'm worried about you. Because I care about you. I'm not going to pretend I know what you're going through. I don't have a clue what it's like to be an addict. To live through the things you've endured. I can only imagine what it's like, and it breaks my heart.

"You're fucked up and that's okay. We all are. Life fucks us all, one way or another. But that doesn't mean you have to go it alone. You don't have to punish and isolate yourself. You've lost so much, but you still have people here who are counting on you. Your clients need you. You inspire them to keep going. You've inspired *me* to keep going."

He stares up at the ceiling, like he's talking to the universe. "I'm tired of losing the people I care about. People I love. I get a tease of what it's like, and then it's ripped away from me. It's a constant reminder that I don't deserve any of it."

"And why is that? Why don't you deserve happiness and love?"

"Never have. I'm not destined for anything more than what I've got."

"That so?" I wave my arm around his apartment. "Look around you. Look at the life you've built. You came from nothing. But you didn't give up. As much as it pains me to say this, Kimmie gave up. Whatever she was going through, she decided to take the easy way out. That's not you. You're more than that. So much more."

"What makes you such an expert?"

"Just calling it like I see it." I cross my arms and narrow my eyes. "Maybe if you let people love you, you wouldn't have to get punched in the face just to feel something other than pain."

He laughs and shakes his head. "Nobody wants this shit show."

"Keep telling yourself that. Let me know how that works out for you." My chair scrapes across the floor as I push away from the table and stand. "Thanks for breakfast."

"Carla, wait." TJ follows me into his bedroom.

"Where are my clothes?"

"They were still wet. I threw them in the dryer."

"Fine. I'm going home. I'll see you later." I swipe my phone off the nightstand and sling my purse over my shoulder.

"Carla," he says, trailing behind me into the hallway.

I spin around, lifting my chin. "What?"

"You don't have any pants on."

I look down at my bare legs sticking out from underneath his oversized T-shirt. "Whatever."

I stomp all the way to the front door and slip into the heels I'd kicked off last night. I know I look ridiculous, but I'm too agitated to care. My apartment is a quick ten minutes away.

Really hoping Mallory is still asleep.

I rip open the door and hesitate, glancing at TJ before I leave. "You're so stubborn for such a smart man, you know that? It baffles me how blind you are when it comes to yourself." I let it slam behind me.

Once I arrive at my apartment, I tiptoe quietly into the living room and shake out of my jacket.

"What on God's green earth are you wearing?"

I jump at the sound of Mallory's voice. She's on the couch eating a bowl of cereal.

I point my index finger at her as a warning. "I had a really shitty night. I need you to save your commentary for another time. I'm taking a shower and then a nap before my shift starts later."

Mallory's bottom lip juts out. "Can I at least take a picture of your ensemble?"

"Do it and I will kill you."

She holds up both hands in surrender. "Okay, okay. No picture. Sheesh. I'm guessing you didn't get laid judging by your crankiness."

"You guessed correctly." I fling my heels into my bedroom and trudge into the bathroom, twisting the knob in the shower all the way to hot.

Chapter Thirty-Four

THE PRESENT

TJ (Fucking finally, right?)

I THOUGHT I WAS IN LOVE BEFORE.

I'd met a stunningly beautiful girl named Merritt. Wild curly hair. Brown eyes, so deep you could get lost in them. The only person who was just as broken as I was.

I thought we could mend our broken parts together. I thought she could be the cure to my lonely life.

But I was wrong.

She wasn't for me to love.

Her heart belonged to another.

So I convinced myself that it would always be this way. Dug my hole even deeper. Prepared myself for a life without love. I'd lost my mom, Woods, Reggie. Nothing good ever stayed for long. I thought I was destined to be alone.

Then Carla walked into that bar.

One look at her in that buttoned-up outfit and I knew I had to have her. Just for one night. I'd indulge myself in the fantasy of a girl like her actually wanting a guy like me.

When our paths crossed a second time, I told myself it was just a coincidence. Like when your friend introduces you to the girl you just boned the night before and you say, "Small world."

Besides, the girl was hung up on her ex and she lived in Florida.

I'd tried to forget about her after that, but she pushed her way into my mind almost every day. Couldn't tell you why. There was something about her. She was stifled. Unaware of the fire she possessed. And like a moth to the flame, I was drawn to her.

When I got the call from Tanner to help move Carla and Mallory into their new apartment, I dropped everything and went.

When she said she needed a job, I made sure she worked for me.

And when I saw that ridiculous bucket list she'd made, I had to help her.

Along the way, I've learned a lot about her. But I've learned even more about myself. Carla has taught me a lot. Coming from the life I've lived, that's not an easy feat.

This woman is caring with the biggest heart out of anyone I've ever known. When Kimmie died, it nearly broke me in half to watch Carla have to go through that kind of loss. I'm used to it. I lose people all the time. Shit, I lost myself for a decade. Reggie saved my life. Carla reminds me a lot of him. I often wonder if he sent her to me. Not sure if it's possible, but it's a nice notion.

I don't believe in destiny. Not anymore. I took control of my life and changed my course. Things don't happen to you because they're part of a plan. That's a victim mentality. Yes, sometimes things happen because of luck. You win the lottery, or you drive over a nail and pop your tire. Shit happens.

But most of the time? Things happen because you let them. I spent a long time letting myself think that I didn't deserve the love of a good woman. I let the shitty people in my life brainwash me into thinking I wasn't worth a damn.

But that's not true.

It took me a while (and a whole lot of therapy) to believe I could be worthy of someone like Carla.

Now I know.

And now I have to tell her.

Chapter Thirty-Five

CARLA

"Sorry! I'm sorry. I hit *snooze* one too many times."

Roger arches a brow. "You're only five minutes later than usual, which means you're still five minutes early for your shift."

I blow a strand of hair out of my face. "Well, I like to be on time."

"Why were you sleeping at three in the afternoon anyway?"

"Didn't get much sleep last night."

"Ah, to be young." Roger ruffles my hair as he walks to the door. "Wait until you have kids."

I ignore the stabbing pain in my stomach. "'Bye, Rog. Enjoy your weekend."

I smooth down my hair and straighten up the desk. Love Roger and all, but he doesn't put anything back where it belongs. Stapler, folders, envelopes, pens. Normally, this makes me laugh. But today? It's another log tossed into my fire.

I don't even know why I'm so angry. Is it the fact that TJ got himself into a dangerous situation last night? He could've been killed. What he did was reckless. Fighting is better than shooting heroin, I suppose, though that's not a very comforting thought.

Part of me is mad at myself. Every time I think I'm getting somewhere with TJ, he slams the door in my face. One step forward, two steps back. First he's hot, then he's cold.

I'm going to need a neck brace after all this whiplash.

Maybe the question is: Why do I care so much?

These thoughts continue to assault my mind for the duration of my shift.

TJ's my boss. Why does it matter what he does in his spare time? If he wants to get beaten to a bloody pulp, so be it. It's not my job to help him with his personal life. Maybe I need to—

"What are you doing?"

A horror movie-worthy scream rips from my throat. "Jesus Christ, TJ! Why are you sneaking up on me like that?"

His lips twitch. "I didn't know I was sneaking up on you. Walked right in your line of vision. Said hi. Thought you saw me."

"Don't laugh. You scared the crap out of me."

"I'm sorry. Didn't realize you were so hard at work." His eyes drop to the stack of papers in my hand. "Think you're good on the staples."

I glance down. The papers I'm holding have a good fifty staples holding them together.

"Stapling is a good way to get out your aggression," I say.

TJ takes my hand. "Come on. I know a better way to get out your aggression."

When I realize he's leading me toward the octagon-shaped boxing ring, I dig my heels and laugh. "Oh, no. I am not getting in that ring."

"Yes, you are."

I cross my arms over my chest, nose in the air. "I won't."

TJ bends forward and hoists me over his shoulder.

"Put me down!"

His chest rumbles against my thighs, and I know he's laughing.

He slips off my sneakers and socks and then tosses them outside the ring before setting me on my feet. Wearing that cocky smirk, he holds his hands up in front of his face, palms facing me. "Hit me."

I roll my eyes and prop my hands on my hips. "Don't be ridiculous. I'm not going to hit you."

"Come on. Afraid you're going to break a nail?"

My hands drop to my sides and ball into fists. "More like I'm afraid I'm going to hurt you."

He grins wide. "Do your best, baby girl. Let's see what you got."

I hurl my fist at his stomach, but he catches it before I make contact. "Atta girl," he says. "Again."

I jab again and follow it up with a left hook, catching him off guard.

He's chuckling as he rubs his shoulder. "Damn, that was a solid punch."

"Good. Now are we done here? I'd like to clock out. Didn't sleep last night and I'm exhausted."

TJ lunges toward me, hooking his arm around my leg, and slams me onto my back in the middle of the ring. With his giant arms wrapped around my body, it didn't hurt. But it sure as hell surprised me.

I squirm to get out from under him, but he presses his pelvis against me and pins my wrists above my head.

This would be really hot if I wasn't so pissed off.

We have a staring match for a good minute before I cave. "What do you want from me?" I ask, chest heaving against his.

"You ran out of my apartment this morning like a bat outta hell. Then I catch you attacking a piece of paper with a stapler. I want you to tell me why you're so mad."

"And I want you to get off me."

He releases my hands and helps me to my feet. "Better?"

"Much." I pace around the ring, thinking of a way to escape this conversation.

"What's going on in that pretty head of yours?"

"I liked you much better when you were locked inside that room every day."

"Want to see what I've been doing in there?"

I falter, coming to a stop in front of him. "You're actually going to show me?"

He nods, gesturing in the direction of the room. "Let's go."

I scoot out of the ring before he has time to change his mind.

I don't know what I expected to see behind that door, but this definitely isn't it.

The floor-to-ceiling mirrors no longer line the walls. A pale blue color and the fresh smell of paint surround us instead, with large windows on the wall to my right. The sunset casts golden streaks onto the wood floor. Several potted plants with large green leaves decorate one corner of the room. An easel is propped up in another corner. And right smack in the middle of the room? A yoga mat.

"What is this?"

TJ's watching me with unwavering intensity. "This is for you."

My head snaps up to meet his eyes. "Me?"

"You are going to teach yoga."

"I can't—"

"And you're going to paint."

"But I—"

"You're going to use this room whenever you want. I made it for you."

"Why?"

He lifts his blocky shoulders and lets them fall. "Because you deserve it." He inches closer to me, reaching out to twirl a lock of my hair. "Because I want to make you happy."

Butterflies swarm my stomach—no, hummingbirds. Their wings flap against my insides, colliding into one another in a frenzy.

My arms wrap around my waist as I step out of TJ's reach. "You know what would make me happy?"

His eyebrows arch. "Apparently not this."

"This," I wave my arms around the room, "is incredible. I'm in shock that you did this. For me. But I didn't need this grand gesture of ... of whatever this is. I'd be happy with the truth. I'd be happy knowing you're okay. I'd be happy if you hadn't put your life in danger like you did last night."

TJ scrubs a hand over his jaw. "I'm sorry you had to see me like that."

"That's what you're sorry for?" I realize I'm yelling, but I can't find the lid to my jar of crazy at the moment. "I had a lot of time to think last night. You know, while I stayed up to make sure you were still breathing and all. I came up with something. Want to hear my theory?"

Amusement flashes on TJ's face. "Please. Enlighten me."

My index finger shoots out at him. "You're a coward. You act like this big, tough macho man. You help everyone and they all sing your praises. But you can't give yourself the same help because you're too scared."

"Scared of what?"

"Feeling," I say louder. "Loving. Trying. Reaching for something you desire, because you're afraid it won't work out. And I get it—believe me, I do. Joe shattered my heart, and losing that baby killed me.

"Do you know what that's like? I had a life inside me. It was a part of me. But in a second, it was gone. Gone like the blood-stained sheets I threw away."

TJ lifts a hand to console me, but I swat it away. "No. I don't need your sympathy. I'm doing just fine. I'm learning to move on and learning to grow from it."

"You are," he says softly. "You are such an incredible force, Carla Evans."

"And so are you." I close the distance between us and cradle his beautiful, bruised face, careful not to press too hard. "You are unstoppable. You can do anything. You just need to believe it. You were the one who told me to let go of the past. But you need to let go of yours. Stop letting your demons dictate your life. Look into your future and plan for something more than what you've got now.

"March into that prison, look your father in the eye, and tell him to go to hell. Find your friend Woods and thank him for being there for you all those years. Fall in love. Get married, have babies—or don't, if that's not what you want, and go on vacation instead. A real vacation with palm trees and clear water.

"Whatever it is that you want in life, all you have to do is reach out and take it."

TJ's hand snakes around my waist, pulling me flush against his body. His sparkling blue eyes are wild, chest expanding with ragged breaths.

"What are you doing?" I ask.

"Taking what I want." Then his lips dive for mine.

His kiss, so possessive, so passionate, breathes life into me. It's an explosion of emotion. I am the flame and he is the wind, whipping around me, driving me to continue burning. The blaze roars, searing everything that exists until there's nothing left but ash and dust. Nothing but a faint memory of what was.

And the only thing you can do with the scorched earth is rebuild. Reforestation.

Start anew.

"I want you, Carla," he murmurs against my mouth. "I want it all with you."

It feels as if all this time I've been standing outside, holding onto a tree, eyes trained on the sky, waiting for the impending dark clouds to roll overhead.

Tonight, it's here.

It's time.

I'm swept up into the eye of the storm. The one that has been building momentum since the first night I laid eyes on this man. The water level's rising. I slip under, and then my heart jumps ship. It flows away as the flood spills out of me.

My heart, once broken and bruised, has now found refuge in the hands of another.

"Take me," I say.

"No." TJ grips my arms and holds me away from him. His eyes are squeezed shut, like he's restraining himself from going any further. "I want more. More than just tonight."

My hands glide over his muscular arms until they reach his chest. I can feel his heart thumping. Hard. It's thunderous. And I know why.

It's rioting. Thrashing against its cage so mine can find its way.

I stretch up onto my toes and make sure he's looking in my eyes when I say, "You have me, TJ. I'm already yours."

My words sound like a shot at the starting line, and our lips fuse together. TJ scoops me up and carries me out into the gym, up the stairs, all the way into his apartment. Our hands are frantic, searching for skin, and when my feet touch the floor in his bedroom, we tear off our clothes.

I watch with hungry eyes as he frees himself from his boxers, taking in every inch of his glorious body. Tattoos and bulging muscles, he's every part the fighter. Strength and intimidation—shoulders wide, chest broad, skin taut over his carved abdomen. But with the bruises and bandages fresh on his skin, he looks more like a warrior than ever before.

The man has been through a lifetime of combat. Raised in a warzone. Battling through every horror imaginable. But standing before me isn't someone who let the war harden him.

No.

Standing before me is a man who slayed all his demons. Tired and beaten, he's laying down his weapons, once and for all. Leaving the past behind him. Starting the next chapter of his life.

He's no longer a gladiator. No longer a slave to the pain. No longer marred by brutality.

He's free.

And I'm going to show him everything he's been missing. Give him everything he deserves.

I pull TJ onto the bed with me and straddle him. He's still in bad shape from last night and I know I need to be careful maneuvering around his wounds, but his fervor is making that a bit difficult. He's grabbing and pulling, licking and biting—and I can't help but meet each of his moves with the same intensity.

We're naked and ready, his hardness, my wetness, and I reach for a condom in his nightstand.

That's when he notices. "You got a tattoo?"

I smile at the surprise in his voice. "I did."

He runs his fingers over the cursive words underlining my left breast: There's always Plan B

His gaze is filled with question and wonderment.

"I wanted your words close to my heart."

His head dips down to touch his lips to the inscription. I feel him smile against my skin when he sees the wildfire of goosebumps spread across the sensitive area.

His eyes meet mine as his tongue heads north and swirls over my nipple. His fingers slip between us and I rock against them when I feel them glide over me.

I'm under his spell as he toys with my body. He drags his lips up my neck, along my jaw, inhaling as he goes. When he reaches my ear, he says, "You better get that condom on me quick."

I tear into the wrapper, roll it over his length, and take him inside me, fast and all at once.

A groan rumbles through him. His hands are on me—those tattooed hands gripping my waist, while I slide him in and out, again and again. He's watching me ride him, wild and raw, and spurred by emotion.

Gathering me in his arms, TJ pulls himself up so he's sitting with his back against his headboard. I wrap my limbs around him, pressing our bodies together, digging my fingers into his massive shoulders as he pumps in and out of me.

"You're so fucking beautiful Carla. So sexy," he whispers. "So perfect." His tongue dips into my mouth and our kiss deepens until we're panting and breathless, suffocating each other with desire and need.

He's thrusting in deep strokes. I'm teetering on the edge, vibration rippling throughout my body, and when I tip over, TJ comes with me. It's a barrage of emotion. I moan his name, my insides clenching around him, body shuddering, as tears brim and roll down my cheeks. I blink through the blurriness so I can catch sight of him coming apart.

Brows pinched together, muscles contracting, lips open to give way for my name. I take it all in as he releases, pleasure and pride whirling inside me.

He nuzzles my cheek but stills when he feels the wet streaks. "What's wrong, my beautiful girl?" He kisses away each salty drop. "Why are you crying?"

I don't give the words time to sit in my mind. I didn't make a list. I haven't thought this through. I don't have a plan.

But the best things in my life happened because I didn't have a plan.

"I'm in love with you."

TJ's eyes close and he rests his forehead against mine. I count the seconds before he answers, terrified that I've said something I shouldn't have.

"God, I was hoping you were," he says. He kisses me with soft and tender lips, and then his eyes open. "Carla, I love you."

"You do?"

He blinds me with a smile, dimples digging into each cheek, eyes sparkling with adoration. "Remember when you told me to fall in love and have babies?"

"Or go on vacation," I add, just to be clear.

He chuckles. "Well, I want to do all of those things with you. I knew it last night. When Tanner brought me home after I'd gotten the shit kicked out of me, and I saw you standing there, it slammed into me harder than any of the hits I'd taken.

"You were there, helping me, nursing my wounds. The way you cared for me, I knew ... I never want anyone to care for me but you. I never want anyone to be at home waiting for me but you. I never want anyone to love me but you." He captures my lips and holds my face close to his. "And I never want to love another for as long as I live. You are the one who was meant for me. I know it. I'm certain of it. I'm going to be the man you deserve."

"You already are that man. You always have been."

We hold each other and kiss, pouring our love into one another, blissful and sweet, floating on a cloud.

Chapter Thirty-Six

TJ

*S*he loves me.

She *loves* me.

Nothing could get better than this feeling, yet I know with Carla, somehow, it will.

She stirs in my arms as the sunrays streak through the window, waking up with a little puddle of drool on my chest.

I can't help but laugh as her eyes go wide before she wipes it away with the sheet.

"Stop," I say, gripping her so she can't go too far. "I want to stay in this moment a little longer."

She settles back down, nuzzling against my neck. Her leg draped over me, body wrapped around mine. "I want to live in this moment."

My fingers drag up and down her bare back. I love that she gets goosebumps every time I touch her. I've never felt this close to anyone before. It scares me as much as it thrills me.

"Remember when I told you my dad killed someone?" There really isn't any other way to segue into this conversation, so I just blurt it out.

She nods and scoots up to lean against the headboard.

I suck in a deep, long breath, then release it through my lips. "The person he killed was my mom."

The shock of that statement consumes her. Every muscle in her body freezes, eyes wide, hands gripping her thighs. The last piece of the puzzle in her mind clicks into place.

"I was thirteen," I continue. "Watched the whole thing. He strangled her and there was nothing I could do."

"Why?" Her voice is barely audible. "Why would he do that?"

"He was a drunk. Always beat on her. That night, things just ... I don't think he even knew what he was doing. I tried to stop him, but ... I couldn't save her."

Her fingers interlace with mine as she lays her head on my shoulder. "How awful it must have been for you to witness that."

I lift her hand to my lips. "It was."

"No wonder you don't want to speak to your father."

"I thought about it. Many times. I don't know what would be worse: He apologizes and is remorseful, or he's still the same piece of shit he always was."

"I think it'd be more difficult to swallow if he regrets it. You'd be faced with the decision to forgive him ... or not."

"I don't know if I have it in me to forgive him."

"Maybe you don't have to. Maybe a person doesn't deserve forgiveness after he does something so heinous."

I press a kiss to Carla's hair, inhaling her sweet scent.

"What do you think about finding Woods?" she asks.

"You know, for so long I held this grudge against him. Like I blamed him for everything that happened to me."

"Because you wanted him to make everything better for you."

I nod. "I'm not sure how I feel now. I guess it's something I have to think about."

"That's a good first step."

Carla's phone vibrates on the nightstand. She glances at the screen and giggles. "Mal's been blowing up my phone. She's going to die when she finds out about us."

I drag her body until she's on top of me, straddling me in complete naked beauty. "And what will you tell her about *us*?"

She lifts a shoulder, avoiding eye-contact with me. "That we kissed."

"And?" I prod her with my morning wood and her eyes close as a moan escapes her lips.

"And that we had sex."

"And?" I brush my thumbs over her nipples, leaning down to take one into my mouth.

"And ... that we're ... in love." She's grinding her hips against me.

"Almost there," I whisper in her ear.

"What else do you want me to tell her?"

"Tell her I'm your boyfriend," I say, continuing to tease her until she's hot and wet.

"I'm your girlfriend?" It's almost a whimper.

"You are." With Carla in my arms, I swing us out of bed and stalk to the shower.

———

I'D ALL BUT BEGGED CARLA TO STAY AND SPEND THE DAY WITH ME. It's Sunday and the gym's closed. I'd made a convincing argument too, making love to every inch of her body. Four times. In four different rooms in my apartment.

Still, Mallory kept calling and Carla wanted to see her face in person when she told her about us.

Us.

I can't stop the dumb grin from spreading across my face every time I think about it.

I'd been prepared to pull out all the stops and prove to her that I could be the kind of man she deserved. I'd built her that yoga slash painting room to show her how much I support and believe in her dreams. I was ready for her to put up a fight. Thought she'd tell me she needed to make one of her lists to help her decide.

But it turns out I didn't need to do any of that. She'd told me she loved me. And she said it first.

I gave her space today, only sending a couple texts throughout the morning, but by lunchtime they'd gone unanswered. Though it was unsettling, I forced myself to keep the negative thoughts at bay.

The negative thoughts that whispered, *Everybody leaves you.*

Everyone you love dies.
You're not good enough for Carla.
She'll realize it soon enough.

I keep busy cleaning the apartment. I'll be asking Carla to move in with me, so now is as good a time as any to make room.

To some people, it might seem like I'm moving fast.

But when you've lived in a realm of torture your entire life, you don't leave the good things to chance when they come along. You hold onto it with everything you've got, and you run with it.

The day continues and I let myself get worried. What if she never made it to her apartment this morning? What if she got into an accident? What if she changed her mind about us?

Without realizing that I'm even doing it, I drive to Carla's place. I release a breath of relief when her car comes into view in the parking lot. Still, I can't ignore the lead ball in the pit of my stomach. Something isn't right.

Mallory answers the door with wide eyes. "Ah, shit."

"Nice to see you too," I say, shouldering past her. "Is Carla here?"

"She ... she's out at the moment."

I stick my head into Carla's room and make my way back into the living room after I see for myself that it's empty. "She has to be here. Her car's here."

"She got picked up."

Mallory's never at a loss for words. Her short sentences signal another warning bell. "Spit it out, Mal. Please. What's going on?"

She releases a groan and her shoulders slump. "She should tell you herself."

Acid pours into my stomach. "Where is she?"

"Don't know. I'm here. With you." She waves her hand in front of my face. "As you can see."

"Did she say anything before she left?"

"That information is also classified."

"Can I do anything to get an answer out of you?"

Her finger taps on her chin. "You could take your shirt off." Her eyes squeeze shut. "Wait! No. That would be wrong now. Damn her, ruining all my fantasies."

"So she told you about us?" I ask, trying to keep this conversation on track. Talking to Mallory is like trying to keep the focus of a puppy when he sees a squirrel dart across the street.

"She did."

"Let me guess: That information is classified as well?"

She shrugs. "You're just going to have to wait for her to get back."

"Awesome."

"Sorry. Chicks before dicks, bro."

I nod, understanding girl code. "Thanks, Mal."

On the way back to my apartment, my thoughts wander to the darkest corners of my mind.

Please don't let this be over before we've even begun.

Chapter Thirty-Seven

CARLA

I thought Mallory called me because I didn't come home last night. I thought she was being her usual dramatic self. I thought she was checking on me like a good friend.

I thought of literally every scenario *except* for this one.

Mallory wore a look of panic when I walked through the apartment door this morning.

"I know, I know. I should've called. But you'll forgive me when I give you all the juicy details of my whereabouts last night." I kick off my shoes and drop my purse onto the floor.

"Uh, Carla," she said. "You have a visitor."

My body froze when I saw him standing there. In my living room. In my apartment. In New York.

Joe.

"You wouldn't answer my calls or texts," he said. "This is my Hail Mary pass."

Leave it to a man to compare our love life to football.

To say I was stunned is an understatement. But that's as far as my emotions went. I wasn't happy. I wasn't angry. Seeing him in front of me after all this time, looking handsome as ever in jeans and a polo shirt, I was numb.

I told him we could go grab coffee and talk. Had to ignore the daggers Mallory shot me. There was no way I'd be able to have a serious talk with her eavesdropping.

On the way to the café, all I could think about was the timing.

Men are like giant toddlers. Picture an adorable kid playing with a toy, claiming it's his favorite. He goes everywhere with it. Eats with it, sleeps with it. He's obsessed with it. When he's had his fill, he tosses it to the side and moves on to the next, cooler toy.

But when another toddler picks up that discarded toy, oh, then the boy pitches a fit. "Mine!" he screams, doing anything and everything to get that toy back.

He only wanted that toy because another kid had it. He didn't really want it back. He just didn't want anyone else to have any fun with it.

Joe's Hail Mary pass is the equivalent of a toddler's temper tantrum. Granted he doesn't know about TJ, but I'd moved on with my life in another city. He hadn't heard from me. His toddler radar told him I was happy without him.

Still, I hear him out. We order our drinks and take a seat at a quiet table in the corner of the café.

He speaks first as I take a sip of my latte. "You look great."

"Thanks. So do you."

"I can't believe you moved here."

"It's not all that different. People here are just ... louder."

He smiles, and my heart pangs. *Stupid heart. Don't go doing that now.*

Joe's hand slides over the table and covers mine. "I've missed you."

I concentrate on our hands touching instead of looking into his eyes. They're the same eyes I used to gaze into for hours on end. The ones I'd seen forever in.

The numbness is subsiding, and old feelings start to seep through. Like a dull ache. Then comes the confusion.

Why do I still feel something for him? Would I always?

"Why?" I ask. "Because you're not with Brianna anymore?"

"Brianna was ... she was a mistake. I was so upset over our breakup and I wasn't thinking straight."

I laugh and retract my hand, keeping it safe on my lap. "You were the one who broke up with me. You left. What were you so upset over?"

"Look, I'll just come right out and say it. I panicked, Carla. I saw that pregnancy test and I panicked. I wasn't ready to have kids. We'd just started college. We had a plan and that wasn't part of the plan. Not yet, anyway. But it doesn't mean I never want to have kids with you. It doesn't mean I don't want to be with you."

And now anger's joining the party. "I got pregnant, Joe. We got pregnant. You abandoned me when I needed you most."

"I know. I regret that more than anything."

"And for what? Because it wasn't part of the plan?"

For the first time, I realize how silly all my plans sounded.

"That's why I'm here," he says. "I need you to know how sorry I am for the way I reacted."

"You can't just tell me to get an abortion and expect everything to go back to normal. We were supposed to be a team, Joe. But the second we were faced with a problem, you went running for the hills. To another woman, might I add."

"Carla, I want to make it up to you. I want you to trust me again. I—"

"No." My voice cracks and I hate that the emotion is getting the best of me. "How can I trust you after what you did? I don't know you anymore."

"Yes, you do." He scoots his chair around the corner of the table until he's beside me, touching my cheek. "You know me better than anyone else."

"I thought I did. But the person I thought you were would've never done this. He would've never ruined us."

Thinking about the person I once knew Joe to be, I can't help but think about the person I used to be. What would the old me have done if Joe had come for me sooner? Would I have gotten back together with him? Would I have given in to my heartache and forgiven his betrayal?

I guess it doesn't matter. I'm not that person anymore.

Sitting here with Joe, I feel different. Everything feels different.

Coming to New York, creating another life for myself, pushing myself outside my comfort zone ... it all changed me.

TJ changed me.

That's how I know I'm making the right decision when I say, "You ruined us, Joe. This isn't something you can fix. I've learned how to live with that. I've moved on. You should too."

———

AFTER I SAY GOODBYE TO JOE AND FILL MALLORY IN ON everything, I race to TJ's apartment.

My phone's dead and Mallory said TJ came looking for me earlier. Not seeing him all day after the night we shared is killing me, and I can't wait to be in his arms again.

When I arrive, I take the stairs two at a time and forgo knocking on his door.

"TJ? Are you here?" I scan the kitchen and living room, and make my way to his bedroom next. "Anybody home?"

I plug my phone into his charger and leave it on his nightstand. I return to the hallway and tap my knuckles against the closed bathroom door. "TJ? You in here?"

I turn the knob and push open the door.

Oh, sweet Jesus.

TJ's soaking in the bathtub with his earbuds in. His giant arm hangs over the side, head tilted back, eyes closed. He looks so peaceful, I take advantage of the stolen moment and allow myself to stare, taking in every perfect part of him.

The swell of his chiseled chest as it meets his collar bone. The curve of his Adam's apple. His prominent jawline. Those perfect, bowed lips. My eyes rove over the world wonder that is this man.

My man.

My warrior.

TJ's eyes open, pinning me with a gaze I can't quite read. His brows are low, jaw clenched.

He doesn't look happy to see me.

"My phone died," I say. "Mal told me you came by."

He pops the buds out and drops them onto the tile. "Was worried about you since I didn't hear from you. Guess you were busy."

"Joe showed up at my apartment this morning. That's why Mal called so many times."

His eyes ignite but his expression remains the same. "And how did that go?"

"As good as can be expected." I shrug. "We talked about what happened and—"

TJ's hand rises to stop me. "Spare me the details."

"Oh." My stomach drops to my feet. Why is he being so cold with me? "Are you okay?"

A smirk tilts the corner of his mouth. "Yeah, I'll be fine. You know me."

My eyebrows collapse. "What does that mean?"

He shakes his head. "Nothing. Just get on with it. Say your goodbye and leave."

"Goodbye?" *Leave?* What on earth ...?

"Aren't you going back with Joe?" he asks.

Ah, there it is. It all clicks into focus. I'd laugh if TJ didn't look so torn up about this.

Go back with Joe? After everything? With the way I feel for TJ? *Ridiculous.*

My teeth drag across my bottom lip as I step out of my shoes. TJ's eyes flick to my hands as I pop the button on my jeans and push them down to the floor. I tug my shirt over my head and snap the clasp on my bra, letting it drop to my feet.

TJ is silent, watching me undress. His eyes slide down my legs, following my panties until they hit the tile. I'm baring myself to him. *For him.*

I step into the tub and settle in with my back to his chest. The water's warm, but it's nothing compared to the heat radiating between our bodies.

"What are you doing?" he whispers, his breath on my ear sending shivers down my spine. His hands remain on the outside of the tub, refusing to touch me.

Refusing to believe that I'd chosen him.

I look over my shoulder and press my lips to his cheek. "I'm taking a bath with my boyfriend."

His throat bobs as he swallows. "But what about ..."

My tongue traces the vein along his neck before I take his earlobe between my teeth. "It's you, TJ. I only want you."

"Are you sure?" His hands slip under the water and caress my thighs.

"Positive."

His hands leave my legs and blaze a trail up my body. They glide over my breasts, bringing the warm water with them. My head drops back on his shoulder as a breathy moan escapes me. He's teasing me in the most sensuous way, swirling his wet fingertips over my nipples, sucking my neck, biting my shoulder, all while grinding his hardness against my back.

"TJ." His name is a whimper on my lips, begging for more.

One hand remains on my chest while his other dips below the water again. He parts my legs and skims his fingers over my center. The water amplifies the sensation he's causing as he slides over my sensitive skin in slow, gentle strokes.

"I love you so much, Carla," he whispers against my ear. "I'm going to take care of you. Make you happy. Make you feel loved."

The only coherent thing I can say is his name, over and over, while he assaults my senses.

"This body is mine," he commands.

"Yours," I say. "I'm yours." I'm writhing in pure agony and bliss under his feather-light touch.

He pushes the tip of his finger inside me while strumming me with his thumb. I'm ready to break apart, and then his hand leaves me. I'm in a daze as he pulls me to my feet and hoists me out of the tub. He carries me to his room and lowers me onto the bed.

He's reaching for a condom when I scoot off the bed. I drop to my knees before him and take him into my mouth. Gripping onto his muscular backside, I drive him in farther, wrapping my tongue around his length. My eyes travel up his taut pelvis, over the rigid lines of his abs, until I meet his fiery gaze.

With his hand wrapped around the back of my neck, he watches me until he's about to explode. He lifts me by my biceps and sets me back on the bed. While he's tearing into the condom, I flip onto my stomach. His eyebrow arches and I flash him a devilish smile.

"God, I love you," he says. He lifts my hips until they're aligned with his and thrusts into me.

TJ hits the best spot from this angle, and his hands are everywhere. Greedy, touching and rubbing every inch of me.

But the thing about TJ is that he doesn't just make love to my body. He makes love to my mind. He might hold my small frame in his hands, but he also possesses my soul.

When we're lying together after, intertwined and satiated, we spend the remainder of the night talking about the future.

Our future.

Chapter Thirty-Eight

TJ

"Thank you for coming with me today."

Carla wraps her scarf around her neck and smiles. "Thank you for taking me." Her lips turn downward as she takes one last look around. "I hate that you were once on the other side of these tables."

I pull her against me and press my lips to the top of her head. "Everything I went through led me to you."

Every Thanksgiving, I volunteer at this soup kitchen in Manhattan. Being here with Carla, serving instead of receiving, is a surreal experience. This doesn't seem like my life. I still feel as if I should be sitting at the table, listening to one of Steve's stories.

I clasp Carla's hand as we walk out the door onto the sidewalk. My eyes bounce off each familiar place we pass, but I don't allow my finger to rise up and point them out. This isn't a happy stroll down memory lane. What would I say? *"There's the alley where I used to scrounge for half-eaten scraps for dinner,"* or, *"That's the warehouse I used to shoot up in."* No. I swallow it down and remind myself that the present no longer has room for my past.

That is, until I spot him.

It's a face I'd recognize anywhere. My spine stiffens and my feet falter, energy spiking through my veins.

"Are you okay?" Carla asks.

It's like seeing a ghost. Unbelievable, though I'm looking right at it. Maybe my mind's playing tricks on me. Or maybe my heart just doesn't want to believe that he's really here.

Could be a mirage. When's the last time I drank water?

"Do you know that man?" Carla whispers.

Nope. Not a mirage. Carla sees him too.

My mouth opens but no sound comes out.

My eyes are fixed on him as he weaves through the crowded sidewalk. He looks exactly like the man I once knew. Only, I don't know him at all. Not anymore.

Anxiety twists my insides as he nears, my heart pounding louder with each step he takes.

I glance down at his shoes.

Still shiny.

"Thomas?" he asks, tearing me out of my dazed stupor.

I nod, still searching for words. A boulder has lodged itself in my throat.

Woods smiles and his arms open wide.

For me.

Carla nudges me toward him until my feet remember how to move. I take three clumsy steps and then his arms are around me.

"My God, I can't believe it's you," Woods says. "I've always wondered what happened to you. I've looked all over this city."

He has?

Woods pulls away and holds me out in front of him. His face is streaked with tears. "Look at you. You're a man now."

Carla clears her throat. "Why don't we grab a cup of coffee? We're kind of taking up the sidewalk here." She gestures at the people stepping around us.

"I'd love to, if that's all right with you." Woods smiles and extends his hand. "I'm Philip Woods."

Carla turns to me, eyes like saucers, before she shakes his hand. "Woods? Oh, my God. It's so nice to meet you. I'm Carla."

"Whaddya say?" he asks, clapping me on the back. "Got some time to sit down and catch up?"

"Sure," I say. "Let's go."

We walk across the street to a small café. Woods keeps looking back over his shoulder at me, like he's afraid to let me out of his sight. I grip Carla's hand like a lifeline.

"This is fate, baby," Carla whispers in my ear. "Just say whatever is in your heart."

Thank God for this woman. I don't know what I did to deserve her, but I am not ever letting go. I place a swift peck on her lips before we enter the café and find a table.

"Order whatever you both want. It's on me," Woods says.

"You don't have to do that." It's the first coherent sentence I'm able to speak. "It'll be my treat."

Woods nods in understanding, a smile spreading on his face. "If you insist."

Woods knows how much it means to me to be able to buy something for him. Even if it's just coffee.

"I don't even know where to start," he says, once we're seated with our drinks. "I have so many questions."

I inhale a deep breath and Carla squeezes my knee under the table. "I was so angry at you for so long. You were the only person I had back then. All I wanted was for you to say you'd take me in. I often think about how different my life would've been had I lived with you."

"I'm so sorry, Thomas. I—"

"It's TJ."

"TJ. Of course." Woods sips his coffee and for the first time, I can see how nervous he is. His hand trembles lifting the cup to his lips. His eyes dart between me and Carla, leg bouncing under the table. You'd never guess he was a badass detective.

"I wish you could know how hard I tried to fight for you to live with me. My wife and I were trying to have kids of our own at that time, and she didn't think it was a good idea to take in a teenager. I tried, because I wanted you to be with me. I always did. I hated watching you go through the things you experienced with your father beating on your mom all those times I was called to your house. And I hated watching you continue to suffer in foster home after foster home. I wish there was something more I could've done."

"I get it. I really do. It took me a long time to come to terms with the fact that it wasn't your fault." I avert my eyes from his, staring into my coffee as if it could give me strength for this conversation. "I blamed you when I should've blamed myself."

Woods shakes his head. "No. You didn't ask for that life. You didn't do anything to deserve it."

"I know that now," I say. "But I made some poor choices. I chose heroin and whiskey. I chose to let my anger rule my life. I got mixed up with the wrong people."

"What happened after you walked out of the precinct that day? Where did you go?"

Now I'm the one overcome with nerves. I'm embarrassed to tell Woods the truth. Embarrassed of myself. But I tell him everything.

Carla wipes her eyes several times as I recount my life, and soon enough I'm handing napkins to Woods too.

"I'm sorry about Reggie," Woods says.

"Me too."

"You know, I checked every hospital and obituary. Not a day went by without wondering where you were. I always hoped to run into you on the street. Always hoped you were doing better."

Carla rests her head on my shoulder. "He is doing so much better than you can imagine."

"I can see that," Woods says with a smile. "He seems lucky to have someone like you in his life."

I gaze down at her just to watch the blush creep onto her cheeks. "What about you? How's your wife?"

"She's well." His eyes drop to the table. "We had our son a year after I last saw you."

"Congratulations. That's great news."

His eyes flick back up to mine. "Named him Thomas."

"You did?"

Carla's reaching for a napkin again.

"I'm proud of you, kid. I'm sorry I wasn't able to help shape you into the man you are now. I'm sorry I couldn't be that person for you."

"I forgive you," I say, choking back tears. "And I hope you can forgive me."

"You know I do." His smile falls. "And I know you don't like to talk about him, but I am sorry about your father. He did an awful thing, but I know what it feels like to lose both your parents, and it isn't easy."

Carla sits up ramrod straight. "What are you talking about?"

His eyes narrow. "Your father ... you don't know?"

I shake my head. "Know what?"

"Your father passed away last month."

"How do you know this?"

"I'd call the jail every once in a while and ask if your old man had any visitors. I was looking for you. A corrections officer, a buddy of mine, said he died. Liver cancer."

I raise my cup. "Good."

"Figured you'd feel that way." Woods checks the time on his watch. "Listen, I can't stay much longer. But I'd like to do this again. Maybe we can exchange numbers." He shrugs. "Make it a regular thing like old times. If you don't want to—"

"We'd love to," Carla says.

I laugh at her eagerness. "Yes. We'd love to."

———

"I HAVE A CONFESSION."

I slip under the comforter and lean against the headboard. "Come lay with me."

Carla wrings her hands together as she paces at the foot of my bed. "I think you're going to be mad."

I raise an eyebrow. "Does this confession have anything to do with Joe?"

"God no." She shakes her head. "Nothing to do with him."

"Okay. Then I won't be mad."

She grimaces and climbs onto the bed. "You won't know that until after you hear my confession."

I stroke her face and press a kiss to her lips. "Talk to me. I promise

I won't be mad."

"Remember when you received that letter from your dad's jail?"

"Yes."

"Remember how you threw it in the garbage?"

"Yes."

"Well ... I may or may not have taken it out of the garbage and saved it for you." Her hands slap against her face as she covers her eyes. "Please don't hate me!"

I struggle to keep a straight face and slide her body closer to me. "And did you read this letter?"

She peeks out from behind her hands. "No. I swear."

"So why keep it?"

"I didn't want you to regret not opening it. But now that he's gone, it might help give you some closure."

"Do you have the letter with you?"

"It's in my notebook."

"Good thing I haven't read your journal lately or I'd have found it."

"Lately?"

I chuckle and reach for her purse on her nightstand.

Her nightstand. Love the sound of that.

I flip through her notebook until I find the envelope. Handing it to her I say, "Go ahead. Read it."

"You want me to read it?"

"Sure. Tell me if there's anything important in there, like some inheritance I don't know about." I cross my arms behind my head and close my eyes.

"Can I read it out loud?"

"Sure, babe. Whatever you want."

She clears her throat as she unfolds the letter. *"To My Son—"*

I crack up laughing.

"TJ," she says. "This is serious. Let me read it before you say anything."

"Fine. Please continue."

"To My Son." She glares at me over the top of the letter.

I mimic zipping my lips and smirk.

"I've been wanting to write you this letter for many years, but to be honest I didn't know what to say. Maybe I'm not sure what you want to hear.

Do you want an apology? I'll give you one.

Will that make everything better? Not one bit.

Do you want me to say I'm a horrible human being? We both know I am.

Would it make you feel better to hear that I've suffered immensely for my sins? Because I have.

The bottom line is: There isn't anything I can say in this letter to make up for what I've done. I killed the only woman who ever loved me. I killed the mother of my child. I put my son through unspeakable hell. I failed you. I failed her.

I failed myself.

I know I can't make you understand why I did what I did. Even I don't understand it. My therapist says that's what happens when you have an addiction. It controls you and you become someone you didn't even know you were capable of being.

I wish I could've been stronger. I wish I could've fought the cravings. Most of all, I wish I could go back. I never meant to hurt your mom. I never meant to hurt you.

But I did. So nothing I say makes a difference.

I'm dying, son. I'm not writing this letter for your sympathy. I'm writing simply to tell you goodbye. Maybe you'll sleep better knowing I finally got the painful death I deserve. Or maybe you don't think about me at all.

I think about you every day. I wonder what your life is like. I wonder what kind of man you've grown into. I wonder if you still look like me.

If you carry any ill feelings towards me, please, let them go. I'm not asking for forgiveness. I don't deserve it. All I'm asking is that you let the past go. I'm sure it hasn't been easy to do after what you witnessed. But the past is an anchor holding you back from moving forward. I don't want you tethered to it.

Goodbye.

-Dad

Carla drops the letter onto the mattress and wipes her cheeks with the backs of her hands. "Wow. That was so ..."

"Pointless?" I say.

"I was going to say *real*. He wasn't begging for forgiveness. He wasn't asking for anything. He just wanted you to lay it all to rest." She sniffles. "That was pretty incredible."

I shrug and toss the letter onto the floor. "For the record, I'm not mad at you for stealing the letter."

She snuggles against me and a small sigh leaves her lips. "What a crazy day. I can't believe we ran into Woods."

"I can't believe his name is Philip."

She giggles. "He named his son after you."

"I know. Crazy, huh?"

"Not crazy. Just another testament to how much of an impact you have on everyone."

We're quiet for a while, lost in our own thoughts.

"Carla?"

"Mhmm."

"I can see it all with you, you know. Everything I never thought I'd get the opportunity to have."

She nuzzles my neck and inhales. "Well, I don't care what happens as long as I'm with you."

"You don't want to make a plan?"

I feel her grin against my skin. "Nope. I don't need one."

The End

EPILOGUE

Five Years Later

FOSTER CHILD. ALCOHOLIC. JUNKIE. HOMELESS. I'VE WORN MANY labels throughout my life, none of them good.

I've been through a lot. Been to the darkest depths of the earth. I've hit rock bottom. Lost every person that ever mattered to me.

It'd be easy to dwell on it, like I did for so long. I remained in my own personal realm of torture. I accepted the shit life handed me. I blamed my father. Blamed Woods. Bobby. Even my mom.

But that's all behind me now.

Now, Carla's all I can see.

I smile at her from where I stand. She's rubbing her belly over the pale pink chiffon bridesmaid dress she's wearing, her dark hair falling in loose waves. I know she's uncomfortable standing all this time in heels, but no one would be able to tell.

That's Carla. She'll do anything for the ones she loves.

Somehow, I've become one of those people. Someone she loves. I'm a lucky bastard. And I don't use that term lightly.

Luck has a lot to do with the things that happen to us. But it's up to us to reclaim the wheel and steer our lives where we want them to go.

Like my buddy Tanner here. He had his issues, sure, but now he's standing at the altar about to marry the love of his life. All because he took responsibility for his actions and owned his shit.

"You may now kiss the bride," says the priest.

Charlotte leans toward Tanner, lips pursed for a clean church kiss— like they practiced. But Tanner's always been a bit of a showoff.

He dips her backward and deepens the kiss until Charlotte's cheeks are as red as her bouquet.

Carla's laughter tears my attention from the newlyweds. I watch her as she watches them, and my heart could not be fuller.

Never thought I'd meet someone like her.

Never thought I'd be days away from becoming a father.

Never thought I'd have anything more than the lonely, empty life I once had.

Carla slips her hand in mine as we walk back down the aisle. "I cannot wait to get these shoes off."

"Why don't we go home? You know Charlotte wouldn't mind under the circumstances."

She shakes her head, as I suspected she would. "I am going to watch my best friend have her first dance with her husband. I am going to dance to exactly two slow songs with you. And I am going to eat cake!"

Two hours later, we've checked off every item on that list except for cake. I'm swaying on the dance floor with Carla wrapped in my arms. Well, there's a giant belly between us, so I'm doing my best to reach her.

Halfway through the song, Carla's body stops moving and her eyes go wide. A gush of water splatters over our shoes.

"But I didn't have cake yet," Carla whines.

"Fuck the cake." I scoop her up and start barreling through the crowd.

An earsplitting scream sounds over the music. "Oh, my God! We're having a baby!" Mallory's shoes clack behind me.

Charlotte beats us to the hall entrance. "Let's take the limo."

Carla shakes her head. "Stay and enjoy the rest of your wedding. Save some cake for me."

"Priorities, Carla. Baby over cake," Mallory says.

Charlotte is reluctant to give in. "Will you call me as soon as he's born?"

"You'll be the first person I call," I say.

"We are not taking the limo," Mallory whispers as we make our way outside. "I'll drive."

Carla looks up at me with a worried expression, and I laugh. "It's either Mal or the douchebag with the red truck. Take your pick."

Carla groans and rests her head on my shoulder.

Mallory rolls her eyes as she climbs into the driver's seat. "I don't know what you're whining about. I'm an expert driver."

The hospital is about fifteen minutes away. Mallory gets us there in eight.

———

AFTER ALL THE CONTRACTIONS, AFTER ALL THE PUSHING AND screaming, we meet our precious bundle of joy.

It's after midnight. Mallory, Charlotte, and Tanner are all passed out in our room, still in their wedding attire. Carla's asleep too.

In the dim light, I gaze down at my sleeping baby boy. Ten tiny fingers and toes. Healthy and strong. Couldn't tell you who he looks like yet. I don't have any of my baby pictures, and he still looks like a wrinkly old man.

As I cradle him in my arms, I'm overcome with emotion. My heart feels so full, I'm shocked my chest hasn't cracked open.

I just can't believe I'm here. In this moment. I witnessed a miracle. And this miracle is for me. *Because* of me.

This is the best thing I've ever done in my life. Loving Carla and creating our child – this is what my struggle was for. This makes it all worth it.

I am finally at peace.

Finally where I'm supposed to be.

I press my lips to my son's tiny head and inhale his perfect scent. "You know, your mom once told me we're all a little bit fucked up," I whisper. "She's right. We've all got our crosses to bear. We all have a past that we lug around like an overstuffed suitcase. You haven't made any mistakes yet, but you will.

"It's hard to let it all go. It's hard to get up and fight. It's hard to change. Grow. Learn. Life's hard. Life isn't fair. You'll learn that. But you can't lie down and give up."

I swipe a tear from my cheek. "I'm going to teach you how to dig deep. You have it in you. We all do. But only some of us choose to use our strength. I want you to know that you have a choice. You *always* have a choice. I'm not a statistic. Not anymore. I'm not a victim. I'm a survivor. I'm a warrior. Your mom is too. And my little man, so are you."

THE END

If you or someone you know needs help dealing with substance abuse, please call the
Substance Abuse & Mental Health Services Administration Hotline:
1-800-662-HELP (4357)

MORE FROM KRISTEN

The Collision Series Box Set with Bonus Epilogue
Collision: Book 1
Avoidance: Book 2, Sequel
The Other Brother: Book 3, Standalone
Fighting the Odds: Book 4, Standalone
Hating the Boss: Book 1, Standalone
Inevitable: Contemporary standalone
What's Left of Me: Contemporary standalone
Dear Santa: Holiday novella
Someone You Love: Contemporary standalone

Want to gain access to exclusive news & giveaways?
Sign up for my monthly newsletter!

Visit my website: https://kristengranata.com/
Instagram: https://www.instagram.com/kristen_granata/
Facebook: https://www.facebook.com/kristen.granata.16
Twitter: https://twitter.com/kristen_granata

Want to be part of my KREW?

Join Kristen's Reading Emotional Warriors
A Facebook group where we can discuss my books, books you're
reading, and where friends will remind you what a badass warrior
you are.

Love bookish shirts, mugs, & accessories?
Shop my book merch shop!

ACKNOWLEDGMENTS

First and foremost, as always, I need to thank my wife. You put up with so much of this "book stuff" and Insta-nonsense, and I couldn't love and appreciate you more. Your support and belief in me is what keeps me going. You are my rock. One day, this will all be worth it—you'll agree when you're sitting on the porch I buy you, "watching the doings."

Mom, you are my biggest fan and I love you for it! If I ever become famous, it will be because of you. Thank you for trying to get my books seen everywhere you go, thank you for reading everything I write, and thank you for helping me on this journey.

Dorthy, you are such an incredible best friend. Thank you for listening to me talk about my books and ideas for hours at a time in the car. Thank you for reading my books, thank you for taking notes as you read each chapter, and thank you for then reading them all over again after I change them. Thank you for your ideas with my stories. Most importantly, thank you for always being there for me.

My Beta babes: Jenn Lockwood, you rock. I love your thoroughness and attention to detail. Becca, your friendship means the world to me and I truly appreciate your help with everything. Mary, you've been invested in TJ's story as much as I have from the beginning. I promised you I'd give him someone worthy with some sass! I appreciate your help, brainstorming, ideas, and friendship. You make me a better writer.

Yasamin: I hope you read this story and realize how strong you are, and how much you are capable of. Don't ever let anyone keep you down because you were meant to fly. Spread those wings and be the badass you ARE!

To all my #bookstagram friends: I appreciate every single like, comment, share, and post. You guys are responsible for getting my books read, and I couldn't keep doing this without your support. You are all warriors. Don't ever forget that!